The Flower of the Chapdelaines

George W. Cable

The Flower of the Chapdelaines

The present edition is a reproduction of previous publication of this classic work. Minor typographical errors may have been corrected without note, however, for an authentic reading experience the spelling, punctuation, and capitalization have been retained from the original text.

ISBN: 978-1-64799-404-4

TABLE OF CONTENTS

I

Next morning he saw her again.

He had left his very new law office, just around in Bienville Street, and had come but a few steps down Royal, when, at the next corner below, she turned into Royal, toward him, out of Conti, coming from Bourbon.

The same nine-year-old negro boy was at her side, as spotless in broad white collar and blue jacket as on the morning before, and carrying the same droll air of consecration, awe, and responsibility. The young man envied him.

Yesterday, for the first time, at that same corner, he had encountered this fair stranger and her urchin escort, abruptly, as they were making the same turn they now repeated, and all in a flash had wondered who might be this lovely apparition. Of such patrician beauty, such elegance of form and bearing, such witchery of simple attire, and such un-Italian yet Latin type, in this antique Creole, modernly Italianized quarter—who and what, so early in the day, down here among the shops, where so meagre a remnant of the old high life clung on in these balconied upper stories—who, what, whence, whither, and wherefore?

In that flash of time she had passed, and the very liveliness of his interest, combined with the urchin's consecrated awe—not to mention his own mortifying remembrance of one or two other-day lapses from the austerities of the old street—restrained him from a backward glance until he could cross the way as if to enter the great, white, lately completed court-house. Then both she and her satellite had vanished.

He turned again, but not to enter the building. His watch read but half past eight, and his first errand of the day, unless seeing her had been his first, was to go one square farther on, for a look at the wreckers tearing down the old Hotel St. Louis. As he turned, a man neat of dress and well beyond middle age made him a suave gesture.

"Sir, if you please. You are, I think, Mr. Chester, notary public and attorney at law?"

"That is my name and trade, sir." Evidently Mr. Geoffry Chester was also an American, a Southerner.

"Pardon," said his detainer, "I have only my business card." He tendered it: "Marcel Castanado, Masques et Costumes, No. 312, rue Royale, entre Bienville et Conti."

"I diz-ire your advice," he continued, "on a very small matter

1

neither notarial, neither of the law. Yet I must pay you for that, if you can make your charge as—as small as the matter."

The young lawyer's own matters were at a juncture where a fee was a godsend, yet he replied:

"If your matter is not of the law I can make you no charge."

The costumer shrugged: "Pardon, in that case I must seek elsewhere." He would have moved on, but Chester asked:

"What kind of advice do you want if not legal?"

"Literary."

The young man smiled: "Why, I'm not literary."

"I think yes. You know Ovide Landry? Black man? Secon'-han' books, Chartres Street, just yonder?"

"Yes, very pleasantly, for I love old books."

"Yes, and old buildings, and their histories. I know. You are now going down, as I have just been, to see again the construction of that old dome they are dim-olishing yonder, of the once state-house, previously Hotel St. Louis. I know. Twice a day you pass my shop. I am compelled to see, what Ovide also has told me, that, like me and my wife, you have a passion for the poétique and the pittoresque!"

"Yes," Chester laughed, "but that's my limit. I've never written a line for print——"

"This writing is done, since fifty years."

"I've never passed literary judgment on a written page and don't suppose I ever shall."

"The judgment is passed. The value of the article is pronounced great—by an expert amateur."

"SHE?" the youth silently asked himself. He spoke: "Why, then what advice do you still want—how to find a publisher?"

"No, any publisher will jump at that. But how to so nig-otiate that he shall not be the lion and we the lamb!"

Chester smiled again: "Why, if that's the point—" he mused. The hope came again that this unusual shopman and his wish had something to do with her.

"If that's the advice you want," he resumed, "I think we might construe it as legal, though worth at the most a mere notarial fee."

"And contingent on—?" the costumer prompted.

"Contingent, yes, on the author's success."

"Sir! I am not the author of a manuscript fifty years old!"

"Well, then, on the holder's success. You can agree to that, can't you?"

"'Tis agreed. You are my counsel. When will you see the manuscript?"

"Whenever you choose to leave it with me."

2

The costumer's smile was firm: "Sir, I cannot permit that to pass from my hand."

"Oh! then have a copy typed for me."

The Creole soliloquized: "That would be expensive." Then to Chester: "Sir, I will tell you; to-night come at our parlor, over the shop. I will read you that!" "Shall we be alone?" asked Chester, hoping his client would say no.

"Only excepting my"—a tender brightness—"my wife!" Then a shade of regret: "We are without children, me and my wife."

His wife. H'mm! She? That amazing one who had vanished within a few yards of his bazaar of "masques et costumes"? Though to Chester New Orleans was still new, and though fat law-books and a slim purse kept him much to himself, he was aware that, while some Creoles grew rich, many of them, women, once rich, were being driven even to stand behind counters. Yet no such plight could he imagine of that bewildering young—young luminary who, this second time, so out of time, had gleamed on him from mystery's cloud. His earlier hope came a third time: "Excepting only your wife, you say? Why not also your amateur expert?"

"I am sorry, but"—the Latin shrug—"that is—that is not possible."

"Have I ever seen your wife? She's not a tallish, slender young——?"

"No, my wife is neither. She's never in the street or shop. She has no longer the cap-acity. She's become so extraordinarily un-slender that the only way she can come down-stair' is backward. You'll see. Well,"—he waved—"till then—ah, a word: my close bargaining—I must explain you that—in confidence. 'Tis because my wife and me we are anxious to get every picayune we can get for the owners—of that manuscript."

Chester thought to be shrewd: "Oh! is she hard up? the owner?"

"The owners are three," Castanado calmly said, "and two dip-end on the earnings of a third." He bowed himself away.

A few hours later Chester received from him a note begging indefinite postponement of the evening appointment. Mme. Castanado had fever and probably la grippe.

II

Early one day some two weeks after the foregoing incident the young lawyer came out of his pension francaise, opposite his office, and stood a moment in thought. In those two weeks he had not again seen Mr. Castanado.

Once more it was scant half past eight. He looked across to the windows of his office and of one bare third-story sleeping-room over it. Eloquent windows! Their meanness reminded him anew how definitely he had chosen not merely the simple but the solitary life. Yet now he turned toward Royal Street. But at the third or fourth step he faced about toward Chartres. The distance to the courthouse was the same either way, and its entrances were alike on both streets.

Thought he as he went the Chartres Street way: "If I go one more time by way of Royal I shall owe an abject apology, and yet to try to offer it would only make the matter worse."

He went grimly, glad to pay this homage of avoidance which would have been more to his credit paid a week or so earlier. His frequent failure to pay it had won him, each time, a glimpse of her and an itching fear that prying eyes were on him inside other balconied windows besides those of the unslender Mme. Castanado.

Temptation is a sly witch. Down at Conti Street, on the courthouse's upper riverside corner, he paused to take in the charm of one of the most picturesque groups of old buildings in the vieux carré. But there, to gather in all the effect, one must turn, sooner or later, and include the upper side of Conti Street from Chartres to Royal; and as Chester did so, yonder, once more, coming from Bourbon and turning from Conti into Royal, there she was again, the avoided one!

Her black cupid was at her side, tiny even for nine years. They disappeared conversing together. With his heart in his throat Chester turned away, resumed his walk, and passed into the marble halls where justice dreamt she dwelt. Up and down one of these, little traversed so early, he paced, with a question burning in his breast, which every new sigh of mortification fanned hotter: Had she seen him?—this time? those other times? And did those Castanados suspect? Was that why Mme. Castanado had the grippe, and the manuscript was yet unread?

A voice spoke his name and he found himself facing the very black dealer in second-hand books.

4

"I was yonder at Toulouse Street," said Ovide Landry, "coming up-town, when I saw you at Conti coming down. I have another map of the old city for you. At that rate, Mr. Chester, you'll soon have as good a collection as the best."

The young man was pleased: "Does it show exactly where Maspero's Exchange stood?" he asked.

Ovide said come to the shop and see.

"I will, to-day; at six." Another man came up, "Ah, Mr. Castanado! How—how is your patient?"

"Madame"—the costumer smiled happily—"is once more well. I was looking for you. You didn't pass in Royal Street this morning."

[Ah, those eyes behind those windows behind those balconies!]

"No, I—oh! going, Landry? Good day. No, Mr. Castanado, I—"

"Madame hopes Mr. Chezter can at last, this evening, come at home for that reading."

"Mr. Castanado, I can't! I'm mighty sorry! My whole evening's engaged. So is to-morrow's. May I come the next evening after? . . . Thank you. . . . Yes, at seven. Just the three of us, of course? Yes."

III

Six o'clock found Chester in Ovide's bookshop.

Had its shelves borne law-books, or had he not needed for law-books all he dared spend, he might have known the surprisingly informed and refined shopman better. Ovide had long been a celebrity. Lately a brief summary of his career had appeared incidentally in a book, a book chiefly about others, white people. "You can't write a Southern book and keep us out," Ovide himself explained.

Even as it was, Chester had allowed himself that odd freedom with Landry which Southerners feel safe in under the plate armor of their race distinctions. Receiving his map he asked, as he looked along a shelf or two: "Have you that book that tells of you—as a slave? your master letting you educate yourself; your once refusing your freedom, and your being private secretary to two or three black lieutenant-governors?"

"I had a copy," Landry said, "but I've sold it. Where did you hear of it? From Réné Ducatel, in his antique-shop, whose folks 'tis mostly about?"

"Yes. An antique himself, in spirit, eh? Yet modern enough to praise you highly."

"H'mm! but only for the virtues of a slave."

Chester smiled round from the shelves: "I noticed that! I'm afraid we white folks, the world over, are prone to do that—with you-all."

"Yes, when you speak of us at all."

"Ducatel's opposite neighbor," Chester remarked, "is an antique even more interesting."

"Ah, yes! Castanado is antique only in that art spirit which the tourist trade is every day killing even in Royal Street."

"That's the worst decay in this whole decaying quarter," the young man said.

"And in all this deluge of trade spirit," Ovide continued, "the best dry land left of it—of that spirit of art—is——"

"Castanado's shop, I dare say."

"Castanado's and three others in that one square you pass every day without discovering the fact. But that's natural; you are a busy lawyer."

"Not so very. What are the other three?"

"First, the shop of Seraphine Alexandre, embroideries; then of Scipion Beloiseau, ornamental ironwork, opposite Mme. Seraphine and next below Ducatel—Ducatel, alas, he don't count; and third, of Placide La Porte, perfumeries, next to Beloiseau. That's all."

"Not the watchmaker on the square above?"

"Ah! distantly he's of them: and there was old Manouvrier, taxidermist; but he's gone—where the spirits of art and of worship are twin." Chester turned sharply again to the shelves and stood rigid. From an inner room, its glass door opened by Ovide's silver-spectacled wife, came the little black cupid and his charge. Ah, once more what perfection in how many points! As she returned to Ovide an old magazine, at last he heard her voice—singularly deep and serene. She thanked the bookman for his loan and, with the child, went out.

It disturbed the Southern youth to unbosom himself to a black man, but he saw no decent alternative: "Landry, I had not the faintest idea that that young lady was nearer than Castanado's shop!"

Ovide shook his head: "You seem yourself to forget that you are here by business appointment. And what of it if you have seen her, or she seen you, here—or anywhere?"

"Only this: that I've met her so often by pure—by chance, on that square you speak of, I bound for the court-house, she for I can't divine where—for I've never looked behind me!—that I've had to take another street to show I'm a gentleman. This very morn'—oh!—and now! here! How can I explain—or go unexplained?"

Ovide lifted a hand: "Will you leave that to my wife, so unlearned yet so wise and good? For the young lady's own sake my wife, without explaining, will see that you are not misjudged."

"Good! Right! Any explanation would simply belie itself. Yes, let her do it! But, Landry——"

"Yes?"

"For heaven's sake don't let her make me out a goody-goody. I haven't got this far into life without making moral mistakes, some of them huge. But in this thing—I say it only to you—I'm making none. I'm neither a marrying man, a villain, nor an ass."

Ovide smiled: "My wife can manage that. Maybe it's good you came here. It may well be that the young lady herself would be glad if some one explained her to you."

"Hoh! does an angel need an explanation?"

"I should say, in Royal Street, yes."

"Then for mercy's sake give it! right here! you! come!" The youth laughed. "Mercy to me, I mean. But—wait! Tell me; couldn't Castanado have given it, as easily as you?"

"You never gave Castanado this chance."

"How do you know that? Oh, never mind, go ahead—full speed."

"Well, she's an orphan, of a fine old family——"

"Obviously! Creole, of course, the family?"

"Yes, though always small in Louisiana. Creole except one New England grandmother. But for that one she would not have been here just now."

"Humph! that's rather obscure but—go on."

"Her parents left her without a sou or a relation except two maiden aunts as poor as she."

"Antiques?"

"Yes. She earns their living and her own."

"You don't care to say how?"

"She wouldn't like it. 'Twould be to say where."

"She seems able to dress exquisitely."

"Mr. Chester, a woman would see with what a small outlay that is done. She has that gift for the needle which a poet has for the pen."

"Ho! that's charmingly antique. But now tell me how having a

7

Yankee grandmother caused her to drop in here just now. Your logic's dim."

"You are soon to go to Castanado's to see that manuscript story, are you not?"

"Oh, is it a story? Have you read it?"

"Yes, I've read it, 'tis short. They wanted my opinion. And 'tis a story, though true."

"A story! Love story? very absorbing?"

"No, it is not of love—except love of liberty. Whether 'twill absorb you or no I cannot say. Me it absorbed because it is the story of some of my race, far from here and in the old days, trying, in the old vain way, to gain their freedom."

"Has—has mademoiselle read it?"

"Certainly. It is her property; hers and her two aunts'. Those two, they bought it lately, of a poor devil—drinking man—for a dollar. They had once known his mother, from the West Indies."

"He wrote it, or his mother?"

"The mother, long ago. 'Tis not too well done. It absorbs mademoiselle also, but that is because 'tis true. When I saw that effect I told her of a story like it, yet different, and also seeming true, in this old magazine. And when I began to tell it she said, 'It is true! My Vermont grand'mère wrote that! It happened to her!'"

"How queer! And, Landry, I see the connection. Your magazine being one of a set, you couldn't let her read it anywhere but here."

"I have to keep my own rules."

"Let me see it. . . . Oh, now, why not? What was the use of either of us explaining if—if——?"

But Ovide smilingly restored the thing to its stack. "Now," he said, "'tis Mr. Chester's logic that fails." Yet as he turned to a customer he let Chester take it down.

"My job requires me," the youth said, "to study character. Let's see what a grand'mère of a 'tite-fille, situated so and so, will do."

Ovide escorted his momentary customer to the sidewalk door. As he returned, Chester, rolling map and magazine together, said:

"It's getting dark. No, don't make a light, it's your closing time and I've a strict engagement. Here's a deposit for this magazine; a fifty. It's all I have—oh, yes, take it, we'll trade back to-morrow. You must keep your own rules and I must read this thing before I touch my bed."

"Even the first few lines absorb you?"

"No, far from it. Look here." Chester read out: "'Now, Maud,'

8

said my uncle—Oh, me! Landry, if the tale's true why that old story-book pose?"

"It may be that the writer preferred to tell it as fiction, and that only something in me told me 'tis true. Something still tells me so."

"'Now, Maud,'" Chester smilingly thought to himself when, the evening's later engagement being gratifyingly fulfilled, he sat down with the story. "And so you were grand'mère to our Royal Street miracle. And you had a Southern uncle! So had I! though yours was a planter, mine a lawyer, and yours must have been fifty years the older. Well, 'Now, Maud,' for my absorption!"

It came. Though the tale was unamazing amazement came. The four chief characters were no sooner set in motion than Chester dropped the pamphlet to his knee, agape in recollection of a most droll fact a year or two old, which now all at once and for the first time arrested his attention. He also had a manuscript! That lawyer uncle of his, saying as he spared him a few duplicate volumes from his law library, "Burn that if you don't want it," had tossed him a fat document indorsed: "Memorandum of an Early Experience." Later the nephew had glanced it over, but, like "Maud's" story, its first few lines had annoyed his critical sense and he had never read it carefully. The amazing point was that "Now, Maud" and this "Memorandum" most incredibly—with a ridiculous nicety—fitted each other.

He lifted the magazine again and, beginning at the beginning a third time, read with a scrutiny of every line as though he studied a witness's deposition. And this was what he read:

IV

THE CLOCK IN THE SKY

"Now, Maud," said uncle jovially as he, aunt, and I drove into the confines of their beautiful place one spring afternoon of 1860, "don't forget that to be too near a thing is as bad for a good view of it as to be too far away."

I was a slim, tallish girl of scant sixteen, who had never seen a slaveholder on his plantation, though I had known these two for years, and loved them dearly, as guests in our Northern home before it was broken up by the death of my mother. Father was an abolitionist, and yet he and they had never had a harsh word between them. If the general goodness of those who do some particular thing were any proof that that particular thing is good to do, they would have convinced me, without a word, that slaveholding was entirely right. But they were not trying to do any such thing. "Remember," continued my uncle, smiling round at me, "your dad's trusting you not to bring back our honest opinion—of anything—in place of your own."

"Maud," my aunt hurried to put in, for she knew the advice I had just heard was not the kind I most needed, "you're going to have for your own maid the blackest girl you ever saw."

"And the best," added my uncle; "she's as good as she is black."

"She's no common darky, that Sidney," said aunt. "She'll keep you busy answering questions, my dear, and I say now, you may tell her anything she wants to know; we give you perfect liberty; and you may be just as free with Hester; that's her mother; or with her father, Silas."

"We draw the line at Mingo," said uncle.

"And who is Mingo?" I inquired.

"Mingo? he's her brother; a very low and trailing branch of the family tree."

As we neared the house I was told more of the father and mother; their sweet content, their piety, their diligence. "If we lived in town, where there's better chance to pick up small earnings," remarked uncle, "those two and Sidney would have bought their freedom by now, and Mingo's too. Silas has got nearly enough to buy his own, as it is."

Silas, my aunt explained, was a carpenter. "He hands your uncle so much a week; all he can make beyond that he's allowed to keep." The carriage stopped at the door; half a dozen servants came, smiling, and I knew Sidney and Hester at a glance, they were so finely different from their fellows.

That night the daughter and I made acquaintance. She was eighteen, tall, lithe and as straight as an arrow. She had not one of the physical traits that so often make her race uncomely to our eyes; even her nose was good; her very feet were well made, her hands were slim and shapely, the fingers long and neatly jointed, and there was nothing inky in her amazing blackness, her red blood so enriched it. Yet she was as really African in her strong, eager mind

10

as in her color, and the English language, on her tongue, was like a painter's palette and brushes in the hands of a monkey. Her first question to me after my last want was supplied came cautiously, after a long gaze at my lighted lamp, from a seat on the floor. "Miss Maud, when was de conwention o' coal-oil 'scuvvud?" And to her good night she added, in allusion to my eventual return to the North, "I hope it be a long time afo' you make dat repass!"

At the next bedtime she began on me with the innocent question of my favorite flower, but I had not answered three other questions before she had placed me where I must either say I did not believe in the right to hold slaves, or must keep silence; and when I kept silence of course she knew. For a long moment she dropped her eyes, and then, with a soft smile, asked if I would tell her some Bible stories, preferably that of "Moses in de boundaries o' Egyp'."

She listened in gloating silence, rarely interrupting; but at the words, "Thus saith the Lord God of Israel, 'Let my people go,'" the response, "Pra-aise Gawd!" rose from her lips in such volume that she threw her hands to her mouth. After that she spoke only soft queries, but they grew more and more significant, and I soon saw that her supposed content was purely a pious endurance, and that her soul felt bondage as her body would have felt a harrow. So I left the fugitives of Egyptian slavery under the frown of the Almighty in the wilderness of Sin; Sidney was trusting me; uncle and aunt were trusting me; and between them I was getting into a narrow corner. After a meditative silence my questioner asked:

"Miss Maud, do de Bible anywhuz capitulate dat Moses aw Aaron aw Joshaway aw Cable buy his freedom—wid money?"

Her manner was childlike, yet she always seemed to come up out of deep thought when she asked a question; she smiled diffidently until the reply began to come, then took on a reverential gravity, and as soon as it was fully given sank back into thought. "Miss Maud, don't you reckon dat ef Moses had a-save' up money enough to a-boughtened his freedom, dat'd a-been de wery sign mos' pleasin' to Gawd dat he 'uz highly fitten to be sot free widout paying?" To that puzzle she waited for no answer beyond the distress I betrayed, but turned to matters less speculative, and soon said good night.

On the third evening—my! If I could have given all the topography of the entire country between uncle's plantation and my native city on the margin of the Great Lakes, with full account of its every natural and social condition, her questions would have wholly gathered them in. She asked if our climate was very hard on

11

negroes; what clothing we wore in summer, and how we kept from freezing in midwinter; about wages, the price of food, what crops were raised, and what the "patarolers" did with a negro when they caught one at night without a pass.

She made me desperate, and when the fourth night saw her crouched on my floor it found me prepared; I plied her with questions from start to finish. She yielded with a perfect courtesy; told of the poor lot of the few free negroes of whom she knew, and of the time-serving and shifty indolence, the thievishness, faithlessness, and unaspiring torpidity of "some niggehs"; and when I opened the way for her to speak of uncle and aunt she poured forth their praises with an ardor that brought her own tears. I asked her if she believed she could ever be happy away from them.

She smiled with brimming eyes: "Why, I dunno, Miss Maud; whatsomeveh come, and whensomeveh, and howsomeveh de Lawd sen' it, ef us feels his ahm und' us, us ought to be 'shame' not to be happy, oughtn't us?" All at once she sprang half up: "I tell you de Lawd neveh gi'n no niggeh de rights to snuggle down anywhuz an' fo'git de auction-block!"

As suddenly the outbreak passed, yet as she settled down again her exaltation still showed through her fond smile. "You know what dat inqui'ance o' yone bring to my 'memb'ance? Dass ow ole Canaan hymn——

"'O I mus' climb de stony hill
Pas' many a sweet desiah,
De flow'ry road is not fo' me,
I follows cloud an' fiah.'"

After she was gone I lay trying so to contrive our next conversation that it should not flow, as all before it had so irresistibly done, into that one deep channel of her thoughts which took in everything that fell upon her mind, as a great river drinks the rains of all its valleys. Presently the open window gave me my cue: the stars! the unvexed and unvexing stars, that shone before human wrongs ever began, and that will be shining after all human wrongs are ended—our talk should be of them.

12

V

At the supper-table on the following evening I became convinced of something which I had felt coming for two or three days, wondering the while whether Sidney did not feel the same thing. When we rose aunt drew me aside and with caressing touches on my brow and temples said she was sorry to be so slow in bringing me into social contact with the young people of the neighboring plantations, but that uncle, on his arrival at home, had found a letter whose information had kept him, and her as well, busy every waking hour since. "And this evening," she continued, "we can't even sit down with you around the parlor lamp. Can you amuse yourself alone, dear, or with Sidney, while your uncle and I go over some pressing matters together?"

Surely I could. "Auntie, was the information—bad news?"

"It wasn't good, my dear; I may tell you about it to-morrow."

"Hadn't I better go back to father at once?"

"Oh, my child, not for our sake; if you're not too lonesome we'd rather keep you. Let me see; has Mingo ever danced for you? Why, tell Sidney to make Mingo come dance for you."

Mingo came; his leaps, turns, postures, steps, and outcries were a most laughable wonder, and I should have begged for more than I did, but I saw that it was a part of Sidney's religion to disapprove the dance.

"Sidney," I said, "did you ever hear of the great clock in the sky? Yes, there's one there; it's made all of stars." We were at the foot of some veranda steps that faced the north, and as she and Mingo were about to settle down at my feet I said if they would follow me to the top of the flight I would tell this marvel: what the learned believed those eternal lamps to be; why some were out of view three-fourths of the night, others only half, others not a quarter; how a very few never sank out of sight at all except for daylight or clouds, and yet went round and round with all the others; and why I called those the clock of heaven; which gained, each night, four minutes, and only four, on the time we kept by the sun.

"Pra-aise Gawd!" murmured Sidney. "Miss Maud, please hol' on tell Mingo run' fetch daddy an' mammy; dey don't want dat sto'y f'om me secon' haynded!" Mingo darted off and we waited. "Miss Maud, what de white folks mean by de nawth stah? Is dey sich a stah as de nawth stah?"

I tried to explain that since all this seeming movement of the

13

stars around us was but our own daily and yearly turning, there would necessarily be two opposite points on our earth which would never move at all, and that any star directly in line with those two points would seem as still as they.

"Like de p'int o' de spin'le on de spinnin'-wheel, Miss Maud? Oh, yass, I b'lieve I un'stand dat; I un'stan' it some."

I showed her the north star, and told her how to find it; and then I took from my watch-guard a tiny compass and let her see how it forever picked out from among all the stars of heaven that one small light, and held quiveringly to it. She hung over it with ecstatic sighs. "Do it see de stah, Miss Maud, like de wise men o' de Eas' see de stah o' Jesus?"

I tried to make plain the law it was obeying.

"And do it p'int dah dess de same in de broad day, an' all day long?—Pra-aise Gawd! And do it p'int dah in de rain, an' in de stawmy win' a-fulfillin' of his word, when de ain't a single stah admissible in de ske-eye?—De Lawd's na-ame be pra-aise'!" Her father, mother, and brother were all looking at it with her, now, and she glanced from one to another with long heavings of rapture.

"Miss Maud," said Silas, in a subdued voice, "dat little trick mus' 'a' cos' you a mint o' money."

"Silas," put in Hester, "you know dass not a pullite question!" But she was ravening for its answer, and I said I had bought it for twenty-five cents. They laughed with delight. Yet, when I told Sidney she might have it, her thanks were but two words, which her lips seemed to drop unconsciously while she gazed on the trinket.

They all sat down on the steps nearest below me, and presently, beginning where I had begun with Sidney, I went on to point out the polar constellations and to relate the age-worn story of Cepheus and Cassiopeia, Andromeda and the divine Perseus.

"Lawd, my Lawd !" whispered the mother, "was dey—was dey colo'd?"

I said two of them were king and queen of Ethiopia, and a third was their daughter.

"Chain' to de rock, an' yit sa-ave at las'!" exclaimed Sidney.

While her husband and children still gazed at the royal stars, Hester spoke softly to me again. "Miss Maud, dass a tryin' sawt o' sto'y to tell to a bunch o' po' niggehs; did you dess make dat up—fo' us?"

"Why, Hester," I said, "that was an old, old story before this country was ever known to white folks, or black," and the eyes of all four were on me as the daughter asked: "Ain't it in de Bi-ible?"

As all but Sidney bade me good night, I heard her say; "I don' care, I b'lieb dat be'n in de Bible an' git drap out by mista-ake!"

14

In my room she grew queerly playful, and continued so until she had drawn off my shoes and stockings. But then abruptly, she took my feet in her slim black hands, and with eyes lifted tenderly to mine, said: "How bu'ful 'pon de mountain is dem wha' funnish good tidin's!" She leaned her forehead on my insteps: "Us bleeged to paht some day, Miss Maud."

I made a poor effort to lift her, but she would not be displaced. "Cayn't no two people count fo' sho' on stayin' togetheh al'ays in dis va-ain worl'," and all at once I found my face in my hands and the salt drops searching through my fingers; Sidney was kissing my feet and wetting them with her tears.

At close of the next day, a Sabbath, my uncle and aunt called all their servants around the front steps of the house and with tears more bitter than any of Sidney's or mine, told them that by the folly of others, far away, they had lost their whole fortune at one stroke and must part with everything, and with them, by sale. Their dark hearers wept with them, and Silas, Hester, and Sidney, after the rest had gone back to the quarters, offered the master and mistress, through many a quaintly misquoted scripture, the consolations of faith.

"I wish we had set you free, Silas," said uncle, "you and yours, when we could have done it. Your mistress and I are going to town to-morrow solely to get somebody to buy you, all four, together."

"Mawse Ben," cried the slave, with strange earnestness, "don't you do dat! Don't you was'e no time dat a-way! You go see what you can sa-ave fo' you-all an' yone!"

"For the creditors, you mean, Silas," said my aunt; "that's done."

Hester had a question. "Do it all go to de credito's anyhow, Miss 'Liza, no matteh how much us bring?" and when aunt said yes, Sidney murmured to her mother, "I tol' you dat." I wondered when she had told her.

Uncle and aunt tried hard to find one buyer for the four, but failed; nobody who wanted the other three had any use for Mingo. It was after nightfall when they came dragging home. "Now don't you fret one bit 'bout dat, Mawse Ben," exclaimed Sidney, with a happy heroism in her eyes that I remembered afterward. "'De Lawd is perwide!'"

"Strange," said my aunt to uncle and me aside, smiling in pity, "how slight an impression disaster makes on their minds!" and that too I remembered afterward.

As soon as we were alone in my chamber, Sidney and I, she asked me to tell her again of the clock in the sky, and at the end of

15

her service and of my recital she drew me to my window and showed me how promptly she could point out the pole-star at the centre of the clock's vast dial, although at our right a big moon was leaving the tree tops and flooding the sky with its light. Toward this she turned, and lifting an arm with the reverence of a priestess said, in impassioned monotone:

> "'De moon shine full at His comman'
> An' all de stahs obey.'"

She kissed my hand as she added good-by. "Why, Sidney!" I laughed, "you mean good night, don't you?"

She bent low, tittered softly, and then, with a swift return to her beautiful straightness, said: "But still, Miss Maud, who eveh know when dey say good night dat it ain't good-by?" She fondled my hand between her two as she backed away, kissed it fervently again, and was gone.

When I awoke my aunt stood in broad though sunless daylight at the bedside, with the waking cup of coffee which it was Sidney's wont to bring. I started from the pillow. "Oh! what—who—wh'—where's Sidney? Why—how long has it been raining?"

"It began at break of day," she replied, adding pensively, "thank God."

"Oh! were we in such bad need of rain?"

"They were—precisely when it came. Rain never came straighter from heaven."

"They?"—I stared.

"Yes; Silas and Hester—and Sidney—and Mingo. They must have started soon after moonrise, and had the whole bright night, with its black shadows, for going."

"For going where, auntie; going where?"

"Then the rain came in God's own hour," she continued, as if wholly to herself, "and washed out their trail."

I sprang from the bed. "Aunt 'Liza!"

"Yes, Maud, they've run away, and if only they may get away. God be praised!"

Of course, I cried like an infant. I threw myself upon her bosom. "Oh, auntie, auntie, I'm afraid it's my fault! But when I tell you how far I was from meaning it——"

"Don't tell me a word, my child; I wish it were my fault; I'd like to be in your shoes. And, I don't care how right slavery is, I'll never own a darky again!"

One day some two months after, at home again with father.

16

Just as I was leaving the house on some errand, Sidney—ragged, wet, and bedraggled as a lost dog—sprang into my arms. When I had got her reclothed and fed I eagerly heard her story. Three of the four had come safely through; poor Mingo had failed; if I ever tell of him it must be at some other time. In the course of her tale I asked about the compass.

"Dat little trick?" she said fondly. "Oh, yass'm, it wah de salvation o' de Lawd 'pon cloudy nights; but time an' ag'in us had to sepa'ate, 'llowin' fo' to rejine togetheh on de bank o' de nex' creek, an' which, de Lawd a-he'pin' of us, h-it al'ays come to pass; an' so, afteh all, Miss Maud, de one thing what stan' us de bes' frien' night 'pon night, next to Gawd hisse'f, dat wah his clock in de ske-eye."

VI

"Landry," Chester said next day, bringing back the magazine barely half an hour after the book-shop had reopened, "that's a true story!"

"Ah, something inside tells you?"

"No need! You remember this, near the end? 'Poor Mingo had failed [to escape]; if I ever tell of him it must be at another time.' Landry, it's so absurd that I hardly have the face to say it; I've got—ha-ha-ha!—I've got a manuscript! and it fills that gap!" The speaker whipped out the "Memorandum"; "Here's the story, by my own uncle, of how the three got over the border and how Mingo failed. I'd totally forgotten I had it. I disliked its beginning far more than I did 'Maud's' yesterday. For I hate masks and costumes as much as Mr. Castanado loves them; and a practical joke—which is what the story begins with, in costume, though it soon leaves it behind—nauseates me. Comical situation it makes for me, this 'Memorandum,' doesn't it—turning up this way?"

Ovide replied meditatively: "To lend it, even to me, would seem as though you sought——"

"It would put me in a false light! I don't like false lights."

"It would mask and costume you."

"Why, not so badly as if I were really in society; as, you know, I'm not! The only place where any man, but especially a society man, can properly seek a girl's society is in society. The more he's worthy to meet her, the more hopelessly—I needn't say hopelessly, but completely—he's cut off from meeting her any other way. Isn't that a gay situation? Ha-ha-ha!"

"You would probably move much in society, even Creole society, without meeting mademoiselle; she has less time for it than you."

"Is that so?"

Cupid, the evening before, had carried a flat, square parcel like a shop's account-books to be written up under the home lamp. Staring at Landry, Chester rather dropped the words than spoke them: "Think of it! The awful pity! For the like of her! Of her! Why, how on earth—? No, don't tell! I know what I'd think of any other man following in her wake and asking questions while hard fortune writes her history. A girl like her, Landry, has no business with a history!"

"Mr. Chester."

"Yes?"

"Has that 'Memorandum' never been printed? I can find out for you, in Poole's Index."

"Do it! It's good enough, and it's named as if to be printed. See? 'The Angel of——'"

"Then why not have Mr. Castanado, while selecting a publisher for mademoiselle's manuscript, select for both?"

Chester shone: "Why—why, happy thought! I'll consider that, indeed I will! Well, good mor'——"

"Mr. Chester."

"Well?"

"Why did you want that new book yesterday?"

"I've met that nice old man the book calls 'the judge,' and he's coaxed me to break my rules and dine with him, at his home uptown, to-night."

"I'm glad. Madame, his wife, was my young mistress when I was a slave. I wish her granddaughter and his grandson—they also are married—were not over in the war—Red Cross. You'd like them—and they would like you."

"Do they know mademoiselle?"

"Indeed, yes! They are the best of her very few friends. But— the Atlantic rolls between."

Chester went out. In the rear door Ovide's wife appeared, knitting. "Any close-ter?" she asked over her silver-bowed spectacles.

"Some," he said, taking down Poole's Index.

She came to his side and they placidly conversed. As she

began to leave him, "No," she said, "we kin wish, but we mustn' meddle. All any of us want' or got any rights to want is to see 'em on speakin' terms. F'om dat on, hands off. Leave de rest to de fitness o' things, de everlast'n' fitness o' things!"

VII

At the Castanados', the second evening after, Chester was welcomed into a specially pretty living-room. But he found three other visitors. Madame, seated on a sort of sofa for one, made no effort to rise. Her face, for all its breadth, was sweet in repose and sweeter when she spoke or smiled. Her hands were comparatively small and the play of her vast arms was graceful as she said to a slim, tallish, comely woman with an abundance of soft, well-arranged hair:

"Seraphine, allow me to pres-ent Mr. Chezter."

She explained that this Mme. Alexandre was her "neighbor of the next door," and Chester remembered her sign: "Laces and Embroideries."

"Scipion," said Castanado to a short, swarthy, broad-bearded man, "I have the honor to make you acquaint' with my friend Mr. Chezter."

Chester pressed the enveloping hand of "S. Beloiseau, Artisan in Ornamental Iron-work."

"Also, Mr. Chezter, Mr. Rene Ducatel; but with him you are already acquaint', I think, eh?"

Chester shook hands with a small, dapper, early-gray, superdignified man, recalling his sign: "Antiques in Furniture, Glass, Bronze, Plate, China, and Jewelry." M. Ducatel seemed to be already taking leave. His "anceztral 'ome," he said, was far up-town; he had dropped in solely to borrow—showing it—the Courrier des Etats-Unis.

That journal, Castanado remarked to Chester as at a corner table he poured him a glass of cordial, brought the war, the trenches, the poilu and the boche closer than any other they knew. Beloiseau and Mme. Alexandre, he softly explained, had come in quite unlooked-for to discuss the great strife and might depart at any moment. Then the reading!

19

But Chester himself interested those two and they stayed. When he said that Beloiseau's sidewalk samples had often made him covet some excuse for going in and seeing both the stock and the craftsman, "That was excuse ab-undant!" was the prompt response, and Castanado put in:

"Scipion he'd rather, always, a non-buying connoisseur than a buying Philistine."

"Come any day! any hour!" said Beloiseau.

Presently all five were talking of the surviving poetry of both artistic and historic Royal Street. "Twenty year' ag-o," said the ironworker, "looking down-street from my shop, there was not a building in sight without a romantic story. My God! for example, that Hotel St. Louis!"

Chester—"had heard one or two of its episodes only the evening before, at that up-town dinner, from a fine old down-town Creole, a fellow guest, with whom he was to dine the next week."

"Aha-a-a! precizely ac-rozz the street from Mme. Alexandre!" said the hostess. "M'sieu' et Madame De l'Isle! Now I detec' that!"

"Have they no son?—or—or daughter?" he asked.

"Not any," Mme. Alexandre broke in with a significant sparkle; "juz' the two al-lone."

"They live over my shop," Beloiseau said. "You muz' know that double gate nex' adjoining me."

"Oh, that lovely piece of ironwork? I took that for a part of your establishment."

"I have only the uze of it with them. My grandpère he made those gate', for the father of Mme. De l'Isle, same year he made those great openwork gate' of Hotel St. Louis. You speak of episode'! One summer, renovating that hotel, they paint' those gate'—of iron openwork—in imitation—mon Dieu!—of marbl'! Ciel! the tragedy of that! Yes, they live over me; in the whole square, both side' the street, last remaining of the 'igh society."

When Mme. Alexandre finally rose to go, and had kissed the upturned brow of her hostess, she went by an inner door and rear balcony. And when Chester and Beloiseau began to take leave their host said to Chester:

"You dine with M. De l'Isle Tuesday. Well, if you'll come again here the next evening we'll attend to—that business."

"Wouldn't that be losing time? I can just as well come sooner."

"No," said madame, "better that Wednesday."

Chester was nettled, but he recovered when the ironworker walked with him around into Bienville Street and at his pension door lamented the pathetic decay of the useful arts and of artistic taste, since the advent of castings and machinery. The pair took such liking for each other's tenets of beauty, morals, art, and life that Chester walked back to the De l'Isle gates, and their parting at last was at the corner half-way between their two domiciles.

Meanwhile madame was saying to her spouse, "Aha! you see? The power of prayer! Ab-ove all, for the he'pless! By day the fo' corner' of my room, by night the fo' post' of my bed, are——"

"Yes, chérie, I know."

"Yes, they're to me for Matthew, Mark, Luke, and John! Since three days every time I heard the cathedral clock I've prayed to them; and now——!"

"Well, my angel? Now?"

"Well, now! He's dining there next Tuesday!"

"Truly. Yet even now we can only hope——"

"Ah, no! Me, I can also continue to supplicate! From now till Wednesday, every time that clock, I'll pray those four évangélistes! and Thursday you'll see—the power of prayer! Oh, 'tis like magique, that power of prayer!"

VIII

On Tuesday evening Chester, a country boy yet now and then, was first at the De l'Isles'.

Madame lauded him. "Punctualitie! tha'z the soul of pleasure!" She had begun to explain why her other guests included but one young lady, when here they came. First, the Prieurs, a still handsome Creole couple whom he never met again. Then that youthful-aged up-town pair, the Thorndyke-Smiths. And last—while Smith held Chester captive to tell him he knew his part of Dixie, having soldiered there in the Civil War—the one young lady, Mlle. Chapdelaine. As Chester turned toward her she turned away, but her back view was enough to startle him.

"Aline," the hostess began as she brought them face to face, but whatever she said more might as well have been a thunderbolt through the roof. For Aline Chapdelaine was SHE.

They went out together. What a stately dining-room! What carvings! What old china and lace on the board, under what soft, rich illumination! The Prieurs held the seats of honor. Chester was

21

on the hostess's left. Mademoiselle sat between him and Mr. Smith. It would be pleasant to tell with what poise the youth and she dropped into conversation, each intensely mindful—intensely aware that the other was mindful—of that Conti Street corner, of Ovide's shop, and of "The Clock in the Sky," and both alike hungry to know how much each had been told about the other. Calmly they ignored all earlier encounter and entered into acquaintance on the common ground of the poetry of the narrow region of decay in which this lovely home lay hid "like a lost jewel."

"Ah, not quite lost yet," the girl protested.

"No," he conceded, "not while the poetry remains," and Smith, on her other hand, said:

"Not while this cluster of shops beneath us is kept by those who now keep them."

"My faith!" the hostess broke in, "to real souls 'tis they are the wonder—and the poésie—and the jewels! Ask Aline!"

"Ask me," Chester said, as if for mademoiselle's rescue; "I discovered them only last week."

"And then also," quietly said Aline, "ask me, for I did not discover them only last week."

M. Prieur joining in enabled Chester to murmur: "May I ask you something?"

"You need not. You would ask if I knew you had discovered them—M. Castanado and the rest."

"And you would answer?"

"That I knew they had discovered you."

"Discovered, you mean, my spiritual substance?"

"Yes, your spiritual substance. That's a capital expression, Mr. Chester, your 'spiritual substance.' I must add that to my English."

"Your English is wonderfully correct. May I ask something else?"

"I can answer without. Yes, I know where you're going to-morrow and for what; to read that old manuscript. Mr. Chester, that other story—of my grand'mére, 'Maud'; how did you like that?"

"It left me in love with your grand'mére."

"Notwithstanding she became what they used to call—you know the word."

"Yes, 'nigger-stealer.' How did you ever add that to your English?"

"My father was one. Right here in Royal Street. Hotel St. Louis. Else he might never have married my—that's too long to tell here."

"May I not hear it soon, at your home?"

22

"Assuredly. Sooner or later. My aunts they are born raconteurs."

"Oh! your aunts. Hem! Do you know? I had an uncle who once was your grandfather's sort of robber, though a Southerner born and bred."

"Yes, Ovide's wife told me. Will you permit me a question?"

"No," laughed Chester, "but I can answer it. Yes. Those four poor runaways to whom your sweet Maud showed the clock in the sky were the same four my uncle helped on—oh, you've not heard it, and it also is too long. I can lend you his 'Memorandum' if you'll have it."

She hesitated. "N-no," she said. "Ah, no! I couldn't bear that responsibility! Listen; Mr. Smith is going to tell a war story of the city."

But no, that gentleman's story was yet another too long for the moment even when the men were left to their cigars. Instead he and Chester made further acquaintance. When they returned to the ladies, "I want you to talk with my wife," said Mr. Smith, and Chester obeyed. Yet soon he was at mademoiselle's side again and she was saying in a dropped voice:

"To-morrow when you're at the Castanados' to read, so privately, would you be willing for Mme. De l'Isle to be there—just madame alone?"

Oh, but men are dull! "I'd be honored!" he said. "They can modify the privacy as they please." Oh, but men are dull! There he had to give place to M. Prieur and presently accepted some kind of social invitation, seeing no way out of it, from the Smiths. So ended the evening. Mlle. Chapdelaine was taken to her home, "close by," as she said, in the Prieurs' carriage.

"They are juz' arround in Bourbon Street, those Chapdelaines," said the De l'Isles to Chester, last to go. "Y'ought to see their li'l' flower-garden. Like those two aunt' that maintain it, 'tis unique. Y'ought to see that—and them."

"I have mademoiselle's permission," he replied.

"Ah, well, then!—ha, ha!" The pair exchanged a smile which seemed to the parting guest to say: "After all he's not so utterly deficient!"

IX

Again the Castanados' dainty parlor, more dainty than ever. No one there was in evening dress, though with its privacy "modified as the Castanados pleased," it had gathered a company of seven.

Chester, not yet come, would make an eighth. Madame was in her special chair. And here, besides her husband, were both M. and Mme. De l'Isle, Mme. Alexandre and Scipion Beloiseau. The seventh was M. Placide Dubroca, perfumer; a man of fifty or so, his black hair and mustache inclined to curl and his eyes spirited yet sympathetic. Just entered, he was telling how consumed with regret his wife was, to be kept away—by an old promise to an old friend to go with her to that wonderful movie, "Les Trois Mousquetaires," when Chester came in and almost at once a general debate on Mlle. Chapdelaine's manuscript was in full coruscation.

"In the firs' place," one said—though the best place he could seize was the seventeenth—"firs' place of all—competition! My frien's, we cannot hope to nig-otiate with that North in the old manner which we are proud, a few of us yet, to con-tinue in the rue Royale. Every publisher——" Mme. Castanado had a quotation that could not wait: "We got to be 'wise like snake' an' innocent like pigeon'!'"

"Precizely! Every publisher approach' mus' know he's bidding agains' every other! Maybe they are honess men, and if so they'll be rij-oice'!"

A non-listener was trying to squeeze in: "And sec'—and sec'—and secon' thing—if not firs'—is guarantee! They mus' pay so much profit in advance. Else it be better to publish without a publisher, and with advertisement' front and back! Tiffany, Royal Baking-Powder, Ivory Soap it Float'! Ten thousand dolla' the page that Ladies' 'Ome Journal get', and if we get even ten dolla' the page—I know a man what make that way three hundred dolla'!"

"He make that net or gross?" some one asked.

"Ah! I think, not counting his time sol-iciting those advertisement', he make it nearly net."

Chester made show of breaking in and three speakers at once begged him to proceed: "How much of a book," he asked Mme. Castanado, "will the manuscript make? How long is it?"

She looked falteringly to her husband: "'Tis about a foot long, nine inch' wide. Marcel, pazz that to monsieur."

24

The husband complied. Chester counted the lines of one of the pages. Madame watched him anxiously.

"Tha'z too wide?" she inquired.

"It isn't long enough to make a book. To do that would take—oh—seven times as much."

"Ah!" Madame's voice grew in sweetness as it rose: "So much the better! So much the more room for those advertisement'!—and picture'!"

"And portrait of mademoiselle!" said Mme. Alexandre, and Mme. De l'Isle smiled assent.

Yet a disappointed silence followed, presently broken by the perfumer: "All the same, what is the matter to make it a pamphlet?"

Beloiseau objected: "No, then you compete aggains' those magazine'. But if you permit one of those magazine' to buy it you get the advantage of all the picture' in the whole magazine."

"Ah!" several demurred, "and let that magazine swallow whole all those profit' of all those advertisement'!"

Chester spoke: "I have an idea—" But others had ideas and the floor besides.

Castanado lifted a hand: "Frien'—our counsel."

Counsel tried again: "I have a conviction that we should first offer this to a magazine—through—yes, of course, through some influential friend. If one doesn't want it another may——"

Chorus: "Ho! they will all want it! That was not written laz' night! 'Tis fivty year' old; they cannot rif-use that!"

"However," Chester persisted, "if they should—if all should—I'd advise——"

"Frien's," Castanado pleaded, "let us hear."

"I should advise that we gather together as many such old narratives as we can find, especially such as can be related to one another——"

"They need not be ril-ated!" cried Dubroca. "We are not ril-ated, and yet see! Ril-ated? where you are goin' to find them, ril-ated?"

"Royal Street!" Scipion retorted. "Royal Street is pave' with old narration'!"

"Already," said Castanado, "we chanze to have three or four. Mademoiselle has that story of her grand'mère, and Mr. Chezter he has—sir, you'll not care if I tell that?—Mr. Chezter has the sequel to that, and written by his uncle!"

"Yes," Chester put in, "but Ovide Landry finds it was printed years ago."

"Proof!" proclaimed Mme. Alexandre, "proof that 'tis good to

25

print ag-ain! The people that read that before, they are mozely dead."

"At the same time," Chester responded, rising and addressing the chair, his hostess, "because that is a sequel to the grand'-mère's story, and because this—this West Indian episode—is not a sequel and has no sequel, and particularly because we ought to let mademoiselle be first to judge whether my uncle's memorandum is fit company for her two stories, I propose, I say, that before we read this West Indian thing we read my uncle's memorandum, and that we send and beg her to come and hear it with us. It's in my pocket."

Patter, patter, patter, went a dozen hands.

"Marcel," the hostess cried in French, "go!"

"I will go with you," Mme. Alexandra proposed, "she will never come without me."

"Tis but a step," said Mme. De l'Isle, "the three of us will go together." They went.

Those who waited talked on of their city's true stories. The vastest and most monstrous war in human history was smoking and roaring just across the Atlantic, and in it they had racial, national, personal interests; but for the moment they left all that aside. "One troub'," Dubroca said, "'tis that all those three stone'—and all I can rim-ember—even that story of M'sieu' Smith about the fall of the city—1862—they all got in them somewhere, alas! the nigger. The publique they are not any longer pretty easy to fascinate on that subjec'."

"Ho!" Beloiseau rejoined, "au contraire, he's an advantage! If only you keep him for the back-ground; biccause in the mind of every-body tha'z where he is, and that way he has the advantage to ril-ate those storie' together and——"

Mademoiselle came. Her arrival, reception, installation near the hostess and opposite Chester are good enough untold. If elsewhere in that wide city a like number ever settled down to listen to an untamed writer's manuscript in as sweet content with one another their story ought to be printed. "Well," Mme. Castanado chanted, "commence." And Chester read:

X

THE ANGEL OF THE LORD

When I was twenty-four I lived at the small capital of my native Southern State.

My parental home was three counties distant. My father, a slaveholding planter, was a noble gentleman, whom I loved as he loved me. But we could not endure each other's politics and I was trying to exist on my professional fees, in the law office of one of our ex-governors. I was kindly tolerated by everybody about me but had neglected social relations, being a black sheep on every hot question of the time—1860.

In the world's largest matters my Southern mother had the sanest judgment I ever knew, and it was from her I had absorbed my notions on slavery. It was at least as much in sympathy for the white man as for the black that she deprecated it, yet she pointed out to me how idle it was to fancy that any mere manumission of our slaves would cure us of a whole philosophy of wealth, society, and government as inbred as it was antiquated.

One evening my two fellow boarders—state-house clerks, good boys—so glaringly left me out of their plan for a whole day's fishing on the morrow, that I smarted. I was so short of money that I could not have supplied my own tackle, but no one knew that, and it stung me to be slighted by two chaps I liked so well. I determined to be revenged in some playful way that would make us better friends, and as I walked down-street next morning I hit out a scheme. They had been gone since daybreak and I was on my way to see a client who kept a livery-stable.

Now, in college, where I had intended to leave all silly tricks behind me, my most taking pranks had been played in female disguise; for at twenty-four I was as beardless as a child.

My errand to the stableman was to collect some part of my fee in a suit I had won for him. But I got not a cent, for as to cash his victory had been a barren one. However, a part of his booty was an old coach built when carriage people made long journeys in their own equipages. This he would "keep on sale for me free of charge," etc.

"Which means you'll never sell it," I said.

Oh, he could sell it if any man could!

I smiled. Could he lend me, I asked, for half a day or so, a good span of horses? He could.

"Then hitch up the coach and let me try it."

He bristled: "What are you going to find out by 'trying' it? What d'you 'llow it'll do? Blow up? Who'll drive it? I can't spare any one."

I was glad. Any man of his would know me, and my scheme called for a stranger to both me and the coach. I must find such a person.

"If I send a driver," I said, "you'll lend me the span, won't you?"

"Oh, yes."

But all at once I decided to do without the whole rig. I went back to my room and had an hour's enjoyment making myself up as a lady dressed for travel. For a woman I was of just a fine stature. In years I looked a refined forty. My hands were not too big for black lace mitts, my bosom was a success, and my feet, in thin morocco, were out of sight and nobody's business. A little oil and a burnt match darkened my eyebrows, my wig sat straight, under the weest of bonnets I wore a chignon, behind one ear a bunch of curls, and, unseen at one side of a modest bustle, my revolver. Though I say it myself, I managed my crinoline with grace.

["That was pritty co'rect," the costumer remarked. "Humph!" said Chester. The three mesdames exchanged glances, and the reading went on.]

XI

Leaving a note on her door to tell our landlady that business would keep me away an indefinite time, I got out at the front gate unobserved, and with a sweet dignity that charmed me with myself walked away under a bewitching parasol, well veiled.

I knew where to find my two sportsmen. A few hundred paces put the town and an open field at my back; a few more down a bushy lane brought me where a dense wood overhung both sides of the narrow way, and the damp air was full of the smell of penny-royal and of creek sands. From here I proposed to saunter down through the woods to the creek, locate my fishermen, and draw them my way by cries of distress.

On their reaching my side my story, told through my veil and between meanings and clingings, was to be that while on a journey in my own coach, a part of its running-gear having broken, I had sent it on to be mended; that through love of trees and wild flowers I had ventured to stay alone meantime among them, and that a snake had bitten me on the ankle. I should describe a harmless one but insist I was poisoned, and yet refuse to show the wound or be borne back to the road, or to let either man stay with me alone while the other went for a doctor, or to drink their whiskey for a cure. On getting back to the road—with the two fellows for crutches—I should send both to town for my coach, keeping with me their tackle and fish. Then I should get myself and my spoils back to our dwelling as best I could and—await the issue. If this poor performance had so come off—but see what occurred instead!

I had shut my parasol and moved into hiding behind some wild vines to mop my face, when near by on the farther side of the way came slyly into view a negro and negress. They were in haste to cross the road yet quite as wishful to cross unseen. One, in home-spun gown and sunbonnet, was ungainly, shoeless, bird-heeled, fan-toed, ragged, and would have been painfully ugly but for a grotesqueness almost winsome.

"She's a field-hand," was my thought.

The other, in very clean shirt, trousers, and shoes, looking ten years younger and hardly full-grown, was shapely and handsome. "That boy," thought I, "is a house-servant. The two don't belong in the same harness. And yet I'd bet a new hat they're runaways."

Now they gathered courage to come over. With a childish parade of unconcern and with all their glances up and down the road, they came, and were within seven steps of me before they knew I was near. I shall never forget the ludicrous horror that flashed white and black from the eyes in that sun-bonnet, nor the snort with which its owner, like a frightened heifer, crashed off a dozen yards into the brush and as suddenly stopped.

"Good morning, boy," I said to the other, who had gulped with consternation, yet stood still.

"Good mawnin', mist'ess."

The feminine title came luckily. I had forgotten my disguise, so disarmed was I by the refined dignity of the dark speaker's mellow voice and graceful modesty. After all, my prejudices were Southern. I had rarely seen negroes, at worship, work, or play, without an inward groan for some way—righteous way—by which our land might be clean rid of them. But here, in my silly disguise, confronting this unmixed young African so manifestly superior to millions of our human swarm white or black, my unsympathetic generalizations were clear put to shame. The customary challenge, "Who' d'you belong to?" failed on my lips, and while those soft eyes passed over me from bonnet to mitts I gave my head as winsome a tilt as I could and inquired: "What is your name?"

"Me?"

"Yes, you; what is it?"

"I'm name', eh, Euonymus; yass'm."

"Oh, boy, where'd your mother get that name?"

"Why, mist'ess, ain't dat a Bible name?"

"Oh, yes," I said, remembering Onesimus. With my parasol I indicated the other figure, sunbonneted, motionless, gazing on us through the brush.

"Has she a Bible name too?"

"Yass'm; Robelia."

Robelia brought chin and shoulder together and sniggered. "Euonymus," I asked, "have you seen two young gentlemen, fishing, anywhere near here?"

"Yass'm, dey out 'pon a san'bar 'bout two hund'ed yards up de creek." The black finger that pointed was as clean as mine.

"You and this woman," thought I again, "are dodging those men." With a smile as of curiosity I looked my slim informant over once more. I had never seen slavery so flattered yet so condemned.

All at once I said in my heart: "You, my lad, I'll help to escape!" But when I looked again at the absurd Robelia I saw I must help both alike.

"Euonymus, did you ever drive a lady's coach?"

"Me? No'm, I never drove no lady's coach."

"Well, boy, I'm travelling—in my own outfit."

"Yass'm."

"But I hire a new driver and span at each town and send the others back."

"Yass'm," said Euonymus. Robelia came nearer.

"My coach is now at a livery-stable in town, and I want a driver and a lady's maid."

"Yass'm."

"I'd prefer free colored people. They could come with me as far as they pleased, and I shouldn't be responsible for their return."

"Yass'm," said Euonymus, edging away from Robelia's nudge.

"Now, Euonymus, I judge by your being out here in the woods this time of day, idle, that you're both free, you and your sister, h'm?"

"Ro'—Robelia an' me? Eh, ye'—yass'm, as you may say, in a manneh, yass'm."

30

"She is your sister, is she not?"

"Yass'm," clapped in Robelia, with a happy grin, and Euonymus quietly added:

"Us full sisteh an' brotheh—in a manneh."

"Umh'm. Could you drive my coach, Euonymus?"

"What, me, mist'ess? Why, eh, o' co'se I kin drive some, but—" The soft, honest eyes, seeking Robelia's, betrayed a mental conflict. I guessed there were more than two runaways, and that Euonymus was debating whether for Robelia's sake to go with me and leave the others behind, or not.

"You kin drive de coach," blurted the one-ideaed Robelia. "You knows you kin."

"No, mi'ss, takin' all roads as dey come I ain't no ways fitt'n'; no'm."

"Well, daddy's fitt'n'!" said the sun-bonnet.

Euonymus flinched, yet smilingly said:

"Yass, da's so, but I ain't daddy, no mo'n you is."

"Well, us kin go fetch him—in th'ee shakes."

Euonymus flinched again, yet showed generalship. "Yass'm, us kin go ax daddy."

I smiled. "Let Robelia go and you stay here."

Robelia waited on tiptoe. "Go fetch him," murmured Euonymus, "an' make has'e."

"Wait! You're a good boy, Euonymus, ain't you?"

"I cayn't say dat, mi'ss; but I'm glad ef you thinks so."

"Y' is good!" said Robelia. "You knows you is!"

"Never mind," I said; "do you belong to—Zion?"

The dark face grew radiant. "Yass'm, I does!"

"Euonymus, how many more of you-all are there besides daddy and mammy?"

The surprise was cruel. The runaway's eyes let out a gleam of alarm and then, as I lighted with kindness, filled with rapt wonder at my miraculous knowledge: "Be'—be'—beside'—beside' d-daddy an' m-mammy? D'ain't no mo', m-mist'ess; no'm!"

"Yass'm," put in Robelia, "da's all; us fo'."

"Just you four. Euonymus, a bit ago I noticed on your sister's ankles some white mud."

"Yass'm." Another gleam of alarm and then a fine, awesome courage. Robelia stared in panic.

"The nearest white mud—marl—in the State, Robelia, is forty miles south of here."

"Is d'—dat so, mist'ess?"

"Yes, and so you also are travellers, Euonymus."

31

"Trav'—y'—yass'm, I—I reckon you mought call us trav'luz, in a manneh, yass'm."

"Well, my next town is thirty miles north of——"

"Nawth!" Euonymus broke in, thinking furiously.

"Now, if instead of hiring just your sister and her daddy I should——"

"Yass'm!"

"Suppose I should take all four of you along, as though you were my slaves——"

"De time bein'," Euonymus alertly slipped in.

"Certainly, that's all. How would that do?"

"Oh, mist'ess! kin you work dat miracle?"

"I can do it if it suits you."

"Lawd, it suit' us! Dey couldn't be noth'n' mo' rep'ehensible!" Robelia vanished. Euonymus gazed into my eyes.

[Had my disguise failed?] "What is it, boy?"

"May I ax you a question, mi'ss?"

"You may ask if you won't tell."

"Oh, I won't tell! Is you a sho' enough 'oman?—Lawd, I knowd you wa'n't! No mo'n you is a man! I seen it f'om de beginnin'!"

"Why, boy, what do you imagine I am?"

"Oh, I don't 'magine, I knows! 'T'uz me prayed Gawd to sen' you. Y' ain't man, y' ain't 'oman! an' yit yo' bofe! Yo' de same what visit Ab'am, an' Lot, an' Dan'l, and de motheh de Lawd!"

"Stop! Stop! Never mind who I am; I've got to put you fifty miles from here before bedtime."

"Yes, my Lawd. Oh, yes, my Lawd!"

"Euonymus! you mustn't call me that!"

"Ain't dat what Ab'am called you?"

"I forget! but—call me mistress!—only!"

"Yass, suh—yass, mi'ss!"

"Good. Now, lad, I can take you alone, horseback, which'll be far swifter, safer, surer——"

A new alarm, a new exaltation—"Oh, no, my—mist'ess; no, no! you knows you on'y a-temptin' o' dy servant!"

"You wouldn't leave daddy and mammy?"

"Oh, daddy kin stick to mammy, an' her to he! but Robelia got neither faith nor gumption, an' let me never see de salvation o' de Lawd ef I cayn't stick by dat—by—by my po' Robelia!"

"But suppose, my boy, we should be mistaken for runaways and tracked and run down."

"Yass'm, o' co'se. Yass'm."

"Can you fight—for your sister?"

32

"Yass, my La'—yass'm, I kin an' I will. I's qualified my soul to' dat, suh; yass'm."

"Dogs?"

"Yass'm, dawgs. Notinstandin' de dawgs come pass me roun' about, in de name o' de Lawd will I lif up my han' an' will perwail."

"Have you only your hands?"

"Da's all David had, ag'in lion an' bah."

"True. Euonymus, I need a man's clothes."

"Yass'm, on a pinch dey mowt come handy."

XII

Here Robelia came again, conducting "Luke" and "Rebecca." Luke's garments were amusingly, heroically patched, yet both seniors were thoroughly attractive; not handsome, but reflecting the highest, gentlest rectitude. One of their children had inherited all that was best from both parents, beautifully exalting it; the other all that was poorest in earlier ancestors. They were evolution and reversion personified.

The father was frank yet deferential. Our parley was brief. His only pomp lay in his manner of calling me madam. I felt myself a queen. Handing him a note to the stable-keeper, "You can read," I said, "can't you? Or your son can?"

"No, madam, I regrets to say we's minus dat."

I hid my pleasure. "Well, at the stable, if they seem to think this note is from a man, or that the coach is owned by a man——"

"Keep silent," put in Euonymus, "an' see de counsel o' de Lawd ovehcome."

Luke went. I pencilled another note. It requested my landlady to give Euonymus a hat, boots, and suit from my armoire and speed him back all she could. (To avoid her queries.)

Rebecca gazed anxiously after this second messenger. Robelia, near by, munched blackberries.

"Rebecca, did you ever think what you'd do if both your children were in equal danger?"

"Why, yass'm, I is studie' dat, dis ve'y day, ef de trufe got to be tol'."

Thought I: "If anything else has to be told, Robelia'll be my

33

only helper." I asked Rebecca which one she would try to save first.

"Why, mist'ess, I could tell dat a heap sight betteh when de time come. De Lawd mowt move me to do most fo' de one what least fitt'n' to"—she choked—"to die. An' yit ag'in dat mowt depen' on de circumstances o' de time bein'."

"Well, it mustn't, Rebecca, it mustn't!"

"Y'—yass'm—no'm'm! Mustn' it?"

"No, in any case you must do as I tell you."

"Oh, o' co'se! yass'm!"

"So promise, now, that in any pinch you'll try first to save your son."

"Yass'm." A pang of duplicity showed in her uplifted glance, yet she murmured again: "Yass'm, I promise you dat." Nevertheless, I had my doubts.

A hum of voices told us my two anglers were approaching, and with Rebecca's quieting hand on the pusillanimous Robelia we drew into hiding and saw them cross the corner of a clearing and vanish again downstream. Then, hearing the coach, we went to meet it.

Both messengers were on the box. Euonymus passed me my bundle of stuff. The coach turned round. Bidding Euonymus stay on the box I had Rebecca and Robelia take the front seat inside. Following in I remarked: "Good boy, that of yours, Luke."

Luke bowed so reverently that I saw Euonymus's belief in me was not his alone. "We thaynk de Lawd," Luke replied, "fo' boy an' gal alike; de good Lawd sawnt 'em bofe."

"Yet extra thanks for the son wouldn't hurt."

Robelia buried a sob of laughter in the nearest cushion, and as we rolled away gaped at me with a face on which a dozen flies danced and played tag. And so we went——.

Chester ceased reading and stood up. For Mlle. Chapdelaine was rising. All the men rose.

"And so, also," she said, "I too must go."

"Oh, but the story is juz' big-inning," Mme. Alexandra protested, and Mme. De l'Isle said:

"I'm sure 'twill turn out magnificent, yes!"

Mademoiselle declared the tale fascinating. She "would be enchanted to stay," but her aunts must be considered, etc.; and when Chester confessed the reading would require another session anyhow Mmes. De l'Isle and Alexandre arose, and M. Castanado asked aloud if there was any of the company who could not return a week from that evening.

No one was so unlucky. "But!" cried Mme. Alexandre, "why not to my parlor?" "Because!" said Mme. Castanado, to Chester's

34

vivid enlightenment, "every week-day, all day, you have mademoiselle with you."

"With me, ah, no! me forever down in my shop, and mademoiselle incessantly upstair'!"

Mme. Castanado prevailed. That same room, one week later.

Scipion and Dubroca escorted Mme. De l'Isle across to her beautiful gates, and Chester, not in dream but in fact, with M. De l'Isle and Mme. Alexandre following well in the rear, walked with mademoiselle to the high fence and green batten wicket of her olive-scented garden in the rue Bourbon. So walking, and urged by him, she began to tell of matters in her father's life, the old Hotel St. Louis life before hers began—matters that gave to "The Clock in the Sky" and "The Angel of the Lord" a personal interest beyond all academic values.

"We'll finish about that another time," she said, and with "another time" singing in his heart like a taut wire he verily enjoyed the rasping of the wicket's big lock as he turned away.

The week wore round. Except M. De l'Isle, kept away by a meeting of the Athénée Louisianais, all were regathered; one thing alone delayed the reading. Each of the three women had separately asked her father confessor how far one might justly—well—lie—to those seeking the truth only for cruel and wicked ends. But as no two had received the same answer, and as Chester's uncle was gone to his reward—or penalty—the question was early tabled. "Well," Mme. Castanado said: "'And so we went—' in the coach. Go on, read."

XIII

And so we went, not through the town but around it.

My attendants were heavy with sleep. Seating Rebecca next me I called Euonymus into the coach and let mother, son, and daughter slumber at ease.

To the few persons we met I paraded my bonnet and curls. Some, in Southern fashion, I questioned. I was a widow who had sold her plantation in order to go and live with a widowed brother. Euonymus too I showed off, who, waking at every halt, presented a face that seemed any boy's rather than a runaway's. So natural to these Africans was the supernatural that I could be one of the men who plucked Lot from Sodom and yet a becurled widow.

When at noon, at a farmhouse, we had fed horses and dined, I at the planter's board, my "slaves" under the house-grove trees, Euonymus took the lines, and for five hours Luke slept inside. Then they changed places again, and Euonymus and I, face to face, watched the long hot day wane, and pass through gorgeous changes into twilight. Often I saw questions in the young eyes that watched me so reverently, but I dared not encourage them; dared not be a talkative angel. Also my brain had its questions. How was I to get out of the most perilous trap into which a sane man—if sane I was— ever thrust himself? There was no sign that we were being pursued, but it was a harrowing puzzle how, without drawing suspicion upon the runaways, to get them once more separated from me and the coach while I should vanish as a lady and reappear as a gentleman.

"Euonymus, boy, if I should by and by dress as a man could you put these woman things on, over what you're wearing, and be a lady in my place?"

"Why, eh, y'—yass'm. Oh, yass'm, ef you say so, my—mistress; howsomever, you know what de good book say' 'bout de Ethiopium."

"Can't change—yes, I know; but this would be only for an hour or two and in the dark."

"It'd have to be pow'ful dahk," sighed Euonymus, and from Robelia's sunbonnet came—"Unh!"

Rebecca interposed: "An' still, o' co'se, we all gwine do ezac'ly what you say."

"Well," I responded, "maybe we won't do that." And we never did. I was still "Mrs. Southmayd," as we came into a small railway station. At the ticket-window I asked if any one had come up in the train of half an hour before, inquiring for a lady in a coach.

"No, ma'am, nobody got off that train. But there's another train at half past eight."

"Oh," I whined, "he won't come on that; he's overrated my speed and gone on to the next station, making five miles more going for me!"

"Why, no, you can give three of your servants a pass to go on with the carriage, keep your maid and wait for the train."

"Ah, no! No lady can choose to travel by rail where she can go in her own coach!"

They said no more except to warn Luke of a bad piece of road about two miles on. Sure enough, in its very middle—crack!—we broke down. "De kingbolt done gone clean in two!" said Luke, and Robelia repeated the news explosively.

"We'll leave the coach," I announced. "Fold the lap-robes on the backs of the two horses, for Rebecca and me. You-all can walk beside us."

After a while, so going, we passed a large plantation house, its windows ruddy with home cheer. A second quarter-mile brought dimly to view a railroad water-tank and an empty flag-station house, and in the next bit of woods I spoke to Euonymus: "Have you that bundle? Ah, yes. Luke, this boy and I are going off here a step for me to change my dress. If any passer questions you, say I'll be right back."

"Yass, madam, but, er, eh—wouldn' you sooner take yo' maid, Robelia, instid?"

"No, for as to dress I'll be as much of a man, when I get back, as Euonymus."

"Is Euonymus gwine change dress too?"

"No, these things that I take off, your wife and Robelia may divide between them."

I started away but Luke lifted a hand. I thought he was going to claim every dud for Robelia. Not so.

"We all thanks you mighty much, madam, but in fac', ef de trufe got to be tol'——"

"It hasn't got to be told me, Luke, if I——"

"Oh, no, madam, o' co'se. I 'uz on'y gwine say—a-concernin' Euonymus——"

I hurried off while the wife chided her good man: "Why don't you dess hide all dem thing' in yo' heart like dey used to do when d' angel 'pear' unto dem?"

Alone with Euonymus, as I whipped off my feminine garb and whirled into the other, I began to say that however suddenly I might leave the fugitives they must rest assured that I was not deserting them. To which——

"Oh, my Lawd," Euonymus replied, "us know dat!"

We reached the pike again. "Rebecca, dismount. Hand me your bridle. Luke, for you-all's better safety I'm going back and return these horses. We may not see one another again——"

"Oh, Lawdy, Lawdy!" moaned Rebecca.

"In dis vain worl' you mean," Luke said.

"That's all. Come, don't waste time. You'd better walk on for a short way in the pike before taking to the woods. Now go all night for all you're worth. Good-by." I turned abruptly. But my led horse was averse to abruptness, and all the family except the torpid Robelia poured up their blessings and rained kisses on my very feet.

In my half-intelligent plan I intended first to stop at the house

37

we had gone by, and had reached the gate of its front lane when I met one of its household, a lad of sixteen, on the pike.

"Yes, he had just seen the disabled coach."

I said that by business appointment with the lady who had just left the coach I had gone to the next railway station northward in order to meet her. That I had come down the turnpike on a hired horse and met her and her servants pushing forward to our appointment as best they could. Now, I said, our business, a law matter, was accomplished and she was gone on on my hired horse. This span I was taking back to the stable whence I had hired them for her in the morning.

The boy's graciousness shamed me through and through. "Why, certainly! He would have the coach drawn up to the house before sunrise and would keep it as long as I liked." He asked me in, but I went on to the little railway town, repeated my tarradiddle at its "hotel," and soon was asleep.

["'Tarradi'l','" said Mme. Castanado, "tha'z may be a species of paternoster, I suppose, eh?"

"No," said Scipion, "I think tha'z juz' a fashion of speech that he took a drink. I do that myself, going to bed."

Chester explained, but said that to admit one's untruthfulness by even a nickname implied some compunction. Whereat two or three put in:

"Ah! if he acknowledge' his compunction he's all right! But we are stopping the story."

It went on.]

XIV

I was awakened, after the breakfast hour, by a tap on my door. Why it gave me consternation I could not have told; I dare say my inveracities of the day before had failed to digest. "Come in," I called, and in stepped my two fishermen.

Their good mornings were pleasant, but, "Fact is," said one, "we're bothered about your client."

"The lady who passed through here last evening?"

"Yes, it looks as though——"

"Go on while I dress. Looks as though—what?"

"As though she wa'n't what you thought, or else——"

I smiled aggressively: "Pardon, I know that lady. 'Or else,' you say? What else? Go on."

"Oh, you go on dressing. Do you know them darkies are hers?"

"Hoh! Are your teeth yours? Why do you ask?"

He handed me a newspaper clipping:

Two Hundred Dollars Reward. Ran away from my plantation in —— county of this State, on the ——— day of ——— the following named and described slaves; father, mother, daughter, and son: . . . A reward of fifty dollars will be paid to any person for the capture and imprisonment in any jail, of each or either of the above named. Etc.

With a laugh I returned the thing and went on dressing. "It doesn't," I said aloud to my busy image in the mirror, "describe my client's darkies at all." I faced round: "Why, gentlemen, if this isn't the most astonishing——"

"Ho-old on. Ho-old on! Finish your dressing. We're told it does describe two of them and we thought we'd just come and see for ourselves."

"And you followed the unprotected lady?"

"We followed four runaway niggers, sir! Else why did they take to the woods inside of a mile from that house where you left the coach? Oh, you're dressed; come along; time's flying!"

Determined to waste all the time I could, "Wait," I said, strapping on my pistol. "Now, gentlemen, we'll follow this matter to the end, beginning now, instantly. But it must be done as——"

"Oh, as privately as possible! Certainly!"

"Certainly. You want the reward and you want it all. But understand, I know you're in error, and I go with you solely to prove you are. Now, by your theory——"

"Oh, come along!" We went. I killed time over my coffee, and in getting a saddle for one of my hired span. "You must excuse us if we're not polite," my friends apologized after another flash of impatience. "Of course those niggers are not on the run in broad day, but their trail's getting cold!"

"You're not as bad-mannered as I am," I laughed as we mounted, but their allusion to hounds made me enjoy the burden of my six-shooter.

As we ambled off, "What were you going to say," one asked me, "about our 'theory,' or something?"

"Oh! I see you think Mrs. Southmayd must have met up with company and left her servants to follow on to the next station alone."

39

"Exactly. We tracked the darkies along the edge of the road; but her horse tracks—we could only see that no horse tracks left the road where any of their man tracks left it."

When we had gone a mile or so one of the boys turned to leave us by a neighborhood road, saying: "I'll rejoin you, 'cross fields, where you turned back last night. I'm going for the dogs."

"Stop! Gentlemen, this is too high-handed. Do you reckon I'll let you run down those four innocent creatures with hounds? I swear you shan't do it, sirs."

"See here," said the one still with me, "come on. We'll show you the very spots where those innocents left the road one by one, and if you don't say they've used every trick known to a nigger to kill their trail, we'll just quit and go home. Does that suit you?"

"Not by a long chalk!" I retorted as I moved with him up the pike. "Those poor simpletons—alone in a strange land, maybe without a pass, at any moment liable to meet a patrol—how easy for them to make the fatal mistake of leaving the road and hiding their tracks!"

"All right, come ahead, you'll see fair play."

We passed the scene of the breakdown and then the house to which the coach had been drawn. I saw the coach in a stable door. By and by a turn in the pike revealed the other clerk and a tall, slim horseman just dismounting among four lop-eared, black-and-brown dogs coupled two and two by light steel breast-yokes. With a heavy whip and without a frown this man gave one of them a quick cut over the face as the brute ventured to lift a voice as hollow and melodious as a bell.

"He's a puppy I'm breaking in," said the man. "Now here, you see"—he pointed to the middle of the road—"is where you, sir, met up with the madam and her niggers, and given her yo' hoss and taken her span. Here's the tracks o' the span, you takin' 'em back; you can see they're the same as these comin' this way. T'other critter's tracks I don't make out, but no matter, here's the niggers' along here—and here, see? and here—here—there." We rode for ten minutes or so. Then halting again:

"Look yonder in that lock o' fence. There's where one went over into the brush."

Beyond the high worm fence grew a stubborn tangle of briers, vines, and cane. "Mind you," I began to call after the nigger-chaser, but one of my companions spoke for me:

"Mr. Hardy, we got to be dead sure they're runaways before we put the dogs on."

"No, we ain't," Hardy called through the back of his head.

"Dandy and Charmer'll tell us if they're not, before we've gone three hundred yards, and I can call 'em off so quick it'll turn 'em a somerset." He dismounted, and, while unyoking the two older hounds, spoke softly a few words of gusto that put them into a dumb ecstasy. One of the boys pressed his horse up to mine.

"There's the place," he said. "Now watch the dogs find it."

As the pair sprang from Hardy's hands one began to nose the air, the other the earth, to left, to right, and to cross each other's short, swift circuits. With stony face while assuming a voice of wildest eagerness he cried in searching whispers: "Niggeh thah, Dandy! Niggeh thah, Charmer! Take him, my lady!"

Skimming the ground with hungry noses, the dogs answered each cry with a single keen yap of preoccupied affirmation. Almost at once Charmer came to the spot pointed out to me, reared her full length upon the rails and let out a new note; long, musical, fretful, overjoyed. Hardy mounted breast-high to the fence's top, wreathed two fingers in the willing brute's collar, lifted her, and dropped her on the other side. There she instantly resumed her search.

At the same time her yoke-mate's deep bay pealed like a trumpet, from a few yards up the roadway. He had struck the broad, frank trail of the other three negroes. The "puppy," still in leash, replied in a note hardly less deep and mellow, but the whip of cool discipline cut him off. From an ox-horn the master blew a short, sharp recall and at once Dandy returned and began his work over, knowing now which runaway to single out. Hardy remained on the fence, watching his favorite, over in the brush. By a stir of the bushes, now here, now there, we could see how busy she was, and every now and then she sent us, as if begging our patience, her eager promissory yelp.

Suddenly her master had a new thought. He stepped onward to the next lock of the fence, scrutinized its top rail, moved to, the next lock, examining the top rail there, then to the next, the next, the next, and at the seventh or eighth beckoned us.

"See, here?" he asked. "Think that ain't a runaway nigger? Look." A splinter had been newly rubbed off the rail. "What you reckon done that, sir; a bird or a fish? That's where he jumped. Look yonder, where he landed and lit out."

The merest fraction of a note from the horn brought the two free dogs to their master, and before he could lift Dandy over the fence Charmer was on the trail. She threw her head high and for the first time filled the resounding timber with the music of her bay.

["Mr. Chester," murmured Mlle. Chapdelaine, and once more

41

he ceased to read. Mme. Castanado had laid her hands tightly to her face. Yet now she smilingly dropped them, saying: "Seraphine— Marcel—please to pazz around that cake an' wine. Well, I su'pose there are yet in the worl'—in Afrique—Asia—even Europe—several kin' of cuztom mo' wicked than that. And still I'm sorry that ever tranzpire. But, Mr. Chezter, if you'll resume?"

Chester once more resumed.]

XV

Hardy's incitements were no longer whispers.

"Dandy! Dandy!" he cried, with wild elation of voice and still no emotion in his face. "Niggeh-fellah thah. Dandy! Ah, Dandy! look him out!"

The music swelled from Dandy's throat. Away went the pair. The younger couple, in yoke, trembled and moaned to be after them. The two clerks had swung down three or four rails from the fence, and with Hardy were hurrying their horses through, when the youngest dog, nose to the ground and tugging his yokemate along, let go a cry of discovery and began to dig furiously under a bottom rail. His master threw him off and drew from under it "Mrs. Southmayd's" tiny beflowered bonnet.

"Good God!" exclaimed one of the boys as he held it up, "they've made way with her!"

"Now, none of that nonsense!" I cried; "she's given it to one of them and they've feared 'twould get them into trouble!" But the three had spurred off and I could only toss it away and follow.

The baying had ceased and an occasional half-smothered yap told that the scent was broken. A huge grape-vine end, hanging from a lofty bough, had enabled the run-away to take a long sidewise swing clear of the ground; but as I came up the brutes had recovered the trail and sped on, once more breaking the still air, far and wide, into deep waves of splendid sound. Close after them, as best they might in yoke, scuttled the younger pair, dragging each other this way and that, their broad ears trailing to their feet, and Hardy riding close behind them, reciting their pedigrees and their distinguishing whims.

Presently we issued from the woods, at the edge of wide fields

42

surrounding a plantation-house and slave-quarters, and I hoped to find the trail broken again; but without a pause the chase turned along a line of fence as if to half encircle the plantation. The master of the hounds, in nervy yet placid words, explained that a runaway knew better than to cross open ground by night and set the house-dogs a-barking. It was only on seeing no workers in the fields that I remembered it was Sunday, and feared intensely that the pious fugitives might have shortened their flight.

From the plantation's farther bound we ran down a long, gentle slope of beautiful open woods. At the bottom of it a clear stream rippled between steep banks shrouded with strong vines. Here the scent had failed and it was wonderful to see the docile faith and intelligence with which the dogs resigned the whole work to their master, and followed beside him while he sought a crossing-place for his horse. This took many minutes, but by and by they scrambled over, he bidding us wait where we were until the dogs should open again; and as he started down-stream along the farther bank the older hounds, at a single word, ran circling out before him in the tangle, electrified by the steel-cold eagerness of his implorings.

But now, to my joy, he found their hungry snufflings as futile as his own scrutinizings and divinations, and after following the stream until my companions fretted openly at the delay, he dropped a note from his horn, rode back with the four dogs, recrossed, and passed down on our side with them at his heels, frowning at last and scanning the tangled growth of the opposite bank.

And now again he came back: "You see, this stream runs so nigh the way they wanted to go that there's no tellin' how fur they waded down it or whether they was two, three, or four of 'em rej'ined together. They're shore to 'a' been all together when they left it, but where that was hell only knows. Come on."

We plunged across after him and followed down the farther bank, and at the point where he had turned back he put the hounds on again. "How do you know there were more than one here?" I asked.

"Because, if noth'n' else, this trail at first was a fool's trail and now it's as smart as cats a-fight'n'—look 'em out, Dandy! Every time the rascals struck a swimmin'-hole they swum it, the men sort o' tote'n' the women, I reckon—ah, my Charmer! Yes, my sweet lady! take 'em! take 'em!"

As the stream emerged into an old field—"Sun's pow'ful hot for you-all!" Hardy added. "Ain't see' such a day this time o' year fo' a coon's age. Hosses feel'n' it. Hard to say which is hottest, sun or brush."

43

We had skirted the branch a full mile, beating its margin thoroughly, and were in deep woods again, when all at once Charmer let out a glad peal. Her mate echoed it and with the stream at their back they were off and away in full cry. The trail was broad and strong and with rare breaks continued so for an hour. Often the dogs made us trot; in open grounds we galloped. Once, in a thickety wet tract where the still air was suffocating and a sluggish runlet meandered widely, Hardy was forced, after long hinderance, to drop the trail and recover it on a rising ground beyond.

There once more we were making good speed when we burst into an open grove where about a small, unpainted frame church a saddle-horse was tied under every swinging limb. Before the church a gang of boys had sprung up from their whittling to be our gleeful spectators. Hardy waved them off with the assurance that we wanted neither their help nor company, and though the trail took us at slackened speed around two sides of the building we passed and were gone while the worshippers were in the first stanza of a hymn started to keep them on their benches.

Noon, afternoon; we made no pause. "It's ketch 'em before night," said Hardy as we bent low under beech boughs, "or not till noon to-morrow."

About mid-afternoon one of the court-house boys, who had been talking softly with the other, turned back with a bare good-by. His friend explained:

"Got to be at his desk early in the morning. But I'm with you till you run 'em down."

Happy for me that he was mistaken. Two hours more were hardly gone when, "My Prince is sick!" he cried, drew in, and under a smoke of his own curses began wildly to unsaddle. Hardy rode on.

"You'll have to get another mount," I said.

"Another hell! I wouldn't leave this horse sick in strange hands for a thousand dollars!" Suddenly he struck an imploring key: "Look here! I'll give you fifty dollars cash to stay with me till I get him out o' this!"

"Five hundred," I called, trotting after Hardy, "wouldn't hire me."

Till I was out of earshot I could hear him damning and cursing me in snorts and shouts as a sneak who would wear my coat of tar and feathers yet, and I was still wondering whether I ought to or not, when I overhauled the nigger-chaser cheering on his dogs. Their prey had again tricked them, and again the cry was, "Take him, Dandy!" and "Hi, Charmer, hi!"

Between shouts: "Is yo' nag gwine to hold out?"

"He's got to or perish," I laughed.

In time we found ourselves under a vast roof of towering pines. The high green grass beneath them had been burned over within a year. The declining sun gilded both the grass and the lower sides of the soaring boughs. Even Hardy glanced back exaltedly to bid me mark the beauty of the scene. But I dared not. The dogs were going more swiftly than ever, and there was a ticklish chance of one's horse breaking a leg in one of the many holes left by burnt-out pine roots. The main risk, moreover, was not to Hardy's trained hunter but to my worn-out livery "nag."

"We've started 'em, all four, on the run," he called, "but if we don't tree 'em befo' they make the river we'll lose 'em after all."

The land began a steady descent. Soon once more we were in underbrush and presently came square against a staked-and-ridered worm fence around a "deadening" dense with tall corn. Charmer and Dandy had climbed directly over it, scampered through the corn, and were waking every echo in a swamp beyond. The younger pair, still yoked, stood under the fence, yelping for Hardy's aid. He sprang down and unyoked them and over they scrambled and were gone, ringing like fire-bells. Outside the fence, both right and left, the ground was miry, yet for us it was best to struggle round through the bushy slough; which we had barely done when with sudden curses Hardy spurred forward. The younger dogs were off on a separate chase of their own. For at the river-bank the four negroes had divided by couples and gone opposite ways.

"Call them back!" I urged. "Blow your horn!" But I was ignored.

XVI

[Chester sat looking at a newly turned page as though it were illegible.

"I'm wondering," he lightly said, "what public enormity of to-day the next generation will be as amazed at as we are at this."

"Ah," Mme. Castanado responded, "never mine! Tha'z but the moral! Aline and me we are insane for the story to finizh!" And the story was resumed, to suffer no further interruption.]

45

At the river we burst out upon a broad, gentle bend up and down which we could see both heavily wooded banks for a good furlong either way.

The sun's last beams shone straight up the lower arm of the bend. On the upper bayed Charmer and Dandy, unseen. On the lower we heard the younger pair. On the upper we saw only the clear waters crinkling in a wide shallow over a gravel-bar, but downstream we instantly discovered Luke and his wife. Silhouetted against the level sunlight, heaving forward with arms upthrown, waist deep in the main current, they were more than half-way across. At that moment two small dark objects, the two dogs, moved out from the shore, after them, each with its wake of two long silvery ripples. The "puppy" was leading.

With a curse their master threw the horn to his lips and blew an imperious note. The rear dog turned his head and would have reversed his course, but seeing his leader keep on he kept on with him. Again the angry horn re-echoed, and the rear dog promptly turned back though the other swam on.

Rebecca threw a look behind and it was pitiful to hear her outcry of despair and terror. But Luke faced about and, backing after her through the flood, prepared to meet the hound naked-handed. Hardy sprang to his tiptoes in the stirrups, his curses pealing across the water. "If you hurt that dog," he yelled, "I'll shoot you dead!"

Up-stream the other two runaways were out on the gravel-bar, Euonymus behind Robelia and Robelia splashing ludicrously across the shoal, tearing off and kicking off—in preparation for deep water—sunbonnet, skirt, waist, petticoat, and howling in the self-concern of abject cowardice.

"Thank heaven, she's a swimmer," thought I, "and won't drown her brother!" For only a swimmer ever cast off garments that way.

The flight of Euonymus, too, was bare-headed and swift, but it was unfrenzied and silent. Neither of them saw Luke or Rebecca; the sun was in their eyes and at that instant Charmer and Dandy, having met some momentary delay, once more bayed joyously and sprang into view. Like Luke, Euonymus faced the brutes. With another fierce outcry Hardy blew his recall of all the four dogs.

Three turned at once but the youngster launched himself at Luke's throat where he stood breast-high in the glassing current. The slave caught the dog's whole windpipe in both hands and went with him under the flood. Hardy's supreme care for Charmer had lost him the strategic moment, but he fired straight at Rebecca.

She did not fall and his weapon flew up for a second shot! but by some sheer luck I knocked the pistol spinning yards away into the river. While it spun I saw other things: Rebecca clasping a wounded arm; Luke and the dog reappearing apart, the dog about to repeat his onset; and Hardy dumb with rage.

"Call the puppy!" I cried, "you'll save him yet."

The master winded his horn, and the dog swam our way. At the same time his fellows came about us, while on the farther bank Luke helped his wife writhe up through the waterside vines, and with her disappeared. Only Euonymus remained in the water, at the far edge of the gravel-bar.

I was so happy that I laughed. "All right," I cried, "I'll pay for the revolver."

Foul epithets were Hardy's reply while he spurred madly to and fro in search of an opening in the vines to let his horse down into the stream. I rode with him, knee to knee. "You'll pay for this with your life !" he yelled down my throat. "I'll kill you, so help me God! Charmer! Dandy! go, take the nigger!"

The whole baying pack darted off for Euonymus's crossing. "Take the nigger, Charmer! Ah! take him, my lady!" We saw that Euonymus could not swim. Still knee to knee with Hardy, I drew and fired. "Puppy's" mate yelped and rolled over, dead.

"Call them back," I said, holding my weapon high; but Hardy only shrieked curses and cried:

"Take the nigger, Charmer, take him!"

I fired again. Poor Dandy! He sprang aside howling piteously, with melting eyes on his master.

"Oh, God!" cried Hardy, leaping down beside the wailing dog, that pushed its head into his bosom like a sick child. "Oh, God, but you shall die for this!"

He was half right but so was I and I checked up barely enough to cry back: "Call 'em off! Call 'em off or I'll shoot Charmer!"

With Dandy clasped close and with eyes streaming he blew the recall. Looking for its effect, I saw Euonymus trying to swim and Charmer quitting the chase. But the young dog kept on. The current was carrying Euonymus away. Twice through vines and brush, while I cried: "Catch the fallen tree below you! Catch the tree!" I tried to spur my horse down into the stream, and on the third trial I succeeded.

The flood had cut the bank from under a great buttonwood. It hung prone over the water, and one dipping fork seized and held the fainting swimmer. The dog was close, but had entered the current too far down and was breasting it while he bayed in protest to his master's horn. Now, as Euonymus struggled along the tree the brute struck for the bank, and the two gained it together. Euonymus ran, but on a bit of open grass dropped to one knee, at bay. The dog sprang. In the negro fashion the runaway's head ducked forward to receive the onset, while both hands clutched the brute's throat. Not dreaming that they would keep their hold till I could get there, I leaped down in the shoal to fire; but the grip held, though the dog's teeth sank into legs and arms, and all at once Euonymus straightened to full stature, lifting the dog till his hind legs could but just tiptoe the ground.

"Right!" I cried; "bully, my boy! Lift him one inch higher and he's whipped!"

But Euonymus could barely hold him off from face and throat.

"Turn him broadside to me!" I shouted, having come into water breast-deep. "Let me put a hole through him!"

But the fugitive's only response was: "Run, Robelia! 'Ever mind me! Run! Run!"

And here came Hardy across the gravel-bar, in the saddle. I aimed at him: "Stand, sir! Stand!"

He hauled in and lifted the horn. Euonymus had heaved the dog from his feet. The horn rang, and with a howl of terror the brute writhed free, leaped into the river and swam toward his master. I sprang on my horse and took the deep water: "Wait, boy! Wait!"

It was hard getting ashore. When I reached the spot of grass I found only the front half of the runaway's hickory shirt, in bloody rags. I spurred to a gap in the bushes, and there, face down, lay Euonymus, insensible. I knelt and turned the slender form; and then I whipped off my coat and laid it over the still, black bosom. For Euonymus was a girl.

XVII

Her eyelids quivered, opened. For a moment the orbs were vacant, but as she drew a deep breath she saw me. Her shapely hand sought her throat-button, and finding my coat instead she turned once more to the sod, moaning, "Brother! Mingo!"

"Is he Robelia?" I asked. "Come, we'll find him."

Clutching my coat to her breast, she staggered up. I helped her put the coat on and sprang into the saddle. "Now mount behind me," I said, reaching for her hand; but with an anguished look:

"Whah Mingo?" she asked. "Is dey kotch Mingo?"

"No, not yet. Your hand—now spring!"

She landed firmly and we sped into the woods.

My merely wounding Dandy was fortunate. It kept Hardy from following me hotfooted or rousing the neighborhood. I dare say he wanted no one but himself to have the joy of killing me.

At a "store" and telegraph-station I let my charge down into a wild plum-patch, bought a hickory shirt, left my half-dead beast, telegraphed my livery-stable client where to find him, and so avoided the complication of being a horse-thief. Then I recovered Euonymus and about ten that night the five of us met on the bank of a creek. Near its farther shore, on a lonely railroad siding, we found a waiting freight-train and stole into one of its empty cars; and when at close of the next day hunger drove us out our pursuers were beating the bush a hundred miles behind.

Fed from a negro-cabin and guided by the stars, we fled all of another night afoot, and on the following day lost Mingo. At broad noon, with an overseer and his gang close by in a corn-field, the seductions of a melon-patch overcame him and he howled away his freedom in the jaws of a bear-trap. His father and mother wept dumb tears and laid their faces to the ground in prayer. Euonymus was frantic. With all her superior sanity, she would not have left the region could she have persuaded us to go on without her.

Well! Day by day we lay in the brush, and night after night fled on. I could tell much about the sweet, droll piety of my three fellow runaways, and the humble generosity of their hearts. No ancient Israelite ever looked forward to the coming of a political Messiah with more pious confidence than they to a day when their whole dark race should be free and enjoy every right that any other race enjoys.

"Even a right to cross two races?" I once asked Luke, smilingly, though with intense aversion.

"No, suh; no, suh! De same Lawd what give' ev'y man a wuck he cayn't do ef he ain't dat man, give' ev'y ra-ace a wuck dey cayn't do ef dey ain't dat ra-ace." I fancy he had been years revolving that into a formula; or—he may have merely heard some master or mistress say it.

"Still," I suggested, "races have crossed, and made new and better ones."

"I don't 'spute dat, suh; no, suh. But de Lawd ain't neveh

49

gwine to make a betteh ra-ace by cross'n' one what done-done e'en-a' most all what even yit been done, on to anotheh what, eh——"

Sidney (Onesimus) put in: "What ain't neveh yit done noth'n'!" And her mother sighed, "Amen!"

XVIII

"Yes?" inquired Mme. Castanado. "Well?"

"Ah, surely!" cried several, "Tha'z not all?"

Mme. De l'Isle appealed to her husband: "Even two, three hun'red mile', that din'n' bring the line of Canada, I think."

"No, but, I suppose, of the Ohio."

"And that undergroun' railway!" said Scipion.

"Yes," Mme. Alexandre agreed, "but that story remain' unfinizh' whiles that uncle of Mr. Chezter couldn' return at his home."

"Not even his State," ventured mademoiselle.

"But he did," Chester said; "he came back."

M. Dubroca spoke up: "Oh, 'tis easy to insert that, at the en'—foot-note."

"And Hardy?" asked Beloiseau, "him and yo' uncle, they di'n' shoot either the other?"

"I believe they did, each the other. I never quite understood the hints I got of it, till now. I know that six months in bed with a back full of somebody's buckshot saved my uncle's life."

"From lynching! That also muz' be insert'!"

Chester thought not. "No, centre the interest in the runaway family, as in mademoiselle's 'Clock in the Sky.'" And so all agreed.

A second time he walked home with mademoiselle, under the same lenient escort as before. One thus occupied, by moonlight, can moralize as he cannot with any larger number. "It's hard enough at best," he said, "for us, in our pride of race, to sympathize—seriously—in the joys, the hopes, the sufferings of souls under dark skins yet as human as ours if not as white."

"Yes, 'tis true. Only one man, Mr. Chester, I ever knew, myself, who did that."

"Your father?"

"Yes, my dear father."

50

"Will you not some day tell me his story?"

"Mr. Castanado will tell you it. Any of those will tell you."

"I can't question them about you, and besides——"

"Well, here is my gate. 'And besides—' what?"

"Besides, why can't you tell me?"

"Ah, I'll do that—'some day,' as you say."

The gate-key went into the lock.

"But, mademoiselle, our 'Clock in the Sky'—our 'Angel of the Lord'—shan't we join them?"

"Ah, they are already one, but you have yet to hear that first manuscript, and that is so very separate—as you will see."

"Isn't it also a story of dark skins?"

"Ah, but barely at all of souls under them; those souls we find it so hard to remember."

"Chère fille"—M. De l'Isle had come up, with Mme. Alexandre—"the three will go gran'ly together! Not I al-lone perceive that, but Scipion also—Castanado—Dubroca. Mr. Chester, my dear sir, the pewblication of that book going to be heard roun' the worl'! Tha'z going produse an epoch, that book; yet same time— a bes'-seller!"

Mademoiselle beamed. "Does Mr. Chester think 'twill be that? A best-seller?"

Chester couldn't prophesy that of any book. "They say not even a publisher can tell."

"Hah!" monsieur cried, "those cunning pewblisher'! they prefer not to tell."

"Some poetry," Chester continued, urged by mademoiselle's eyes, "doesn't pay the poets over a few thousand a year—per volume; while some novels pay their authors—well—fortunes."

"That they go," madame broke in, "and buy some palaces in Italie! And tha'z but the biginning; you have not count' the dramatization—hundreds the week! and those movie'—the same! and those tranzlation'!"

"Well, I think we will be satisfied, Mr. Chester, with the tenth of that, eh?"

Chester's reply was drowned in monsieur's: "No, my child! But nine-tenth' maybe, yes! No-no-no! if those pewblisher' find out you are satisfi' by one-tenth, one-tenth is all you'll ever see!"

"Ah," said mademoiselle to madame, "even the one-tenth I mustn't tell to my aunts. They wouldn't sleep to-night. And myself— 'publication, dramatization, movies, translation'—I believe I'll lie awake till daylight, making that into a song—a hymn!"

A wonderful sight she was, pausing in the open gate, with the little high-fenced garden at her back, a street-lamp lighting her face.

51

Chester harked back to that first manuscript. It "ought not to wait another week," he declared.

"No," monsieur said, "and since we all have read that egcept only you."

Chester looked to mademoiselle: "Then I suppose I might read it with the Castanados alone."

"No," madame put in, "you see, you can't riturn at Castanado's immediately to-morrow or next day. That next day, tha'z Sunday, but you don't know if madame goin' to have the stren'th for that fati-gue. Yet same time you can't wait forever! And bisside', yo' Aunt Corinne, Aunt Yvonne—Mr. Chezter he's never have that lugsury to meet them, and that will be a very choice o'casion for Mr. Chezter to do that, if——"

"If he'll take the pains," the niece broke in, "to call Sunday afternoon. Then I'll have the manuscript back from Mr. Castanado and we'll read it to my Aunt Corinne and my Aunt Yvonne, all four together in the garden."

"Yes, yet not in this li'l' garden in the front, but in the large, far back from the house, in the h-arbor of 'oneysuckle and by the side of the li'l' lake, eh?" So prompted madame.

"Assuredly," said the smiling girl; "not in the front, where is no room for a place to sit down!"

Chester's acceptance was eager. Then once more the batten gate closed and the key grated between him and Aline—marvellous, marvellous Aline Chapdelaine.

XIX

The sunbeams of a tedious Sabbath began noticeably to slant.

For two days, night, morning, noon, and afternoon, Geoffry Chester had silently speculated on what he was to see, hear, and otherwise experience when, as early as he might in keeping with the Chapdelaine dignity and his, he should pull the tiny brass bell-knob on their tall gate-post.

Chapdelaine! Impressive, patrician title. Impressive too those baptismal names; implying a refinement invincible in the vale of adversity. Killing time up one street and down another—Rampart, Ursuline, Burgundy—he pictured personalities to fit them: for

Corinne a presence stately in advanced years and preserved beauty; for Yvonne a fragile form suggestive of mother-o'-pearl, of antique lace. Knowledge of Aline justified such inferences—within bounds. With other charms she had all these, and must have got them from ancestral sources as truly Mlle. Corinne's and Mlle. Yvonne's as hers.

"Oh, of course," he pondered, "there are contrary possibilities. They may easily fall short, far short, of her, in outer graces, and show their kinship only in a reflection of her inner fineness. They may be no more surprising than those dear old De l'Isles, or the Prieurs, or than Mrs. Thorndyke-Smith. So let it be! Aline——"

"Aline-Aline!" alarmingly echoed his heart.

"Aline is enough." Enough? Alas, too much! He felt himself far too forthpushing in—he would not confess more—a solicitude for her which he could not stifle; an inextinguishable wish to disentangle her from the officious care of those by whom she was surrounded—encumbered. "I've no right to this state of mind," he thought; "none." He reached the gate. He rang.

A footfall of daintiest lightness came running! ["Aline-Aline!"] So might Allegro have tripped it. The key rasped round, ["Aline-Aline!"] the portal drew in, and he found himself getting his first front view of Cupid, the small black satellite.

A pleasing object. Smaller than ever. White-collared as ever, starched and brushed to the sheen of a new penny and ugly of face as a gargoyle—ugly as his goddess was beautiful. Not merely negroidal, in lips, nose, ears, and tight black wool divided on the absolute equator; not racially but uniquely ugly—till he smiled—and spoke. He smiled and spoke with a joy of soul, a transparency of innocence, a rapture of love, that made his ugliness positively endearing even apart from the entranced recognition they radiated.

"Ladies at home? Yassuh," he said, with an ecstasy as if he announced the world's war suddenly over, all oceans safe, all peoples free. He led the way up the cramped white-shell walk with a ceremonial precision that gave the caller time to notice the garden. It was hardly an empire. It lay on either side in two right-angled figures, each, say, of sixty by fourteen feet, every foot repeating florally the smile of the child. The rigid beds were curbed with brick water-painted as red as Cupid's gums. The three fences were green with vines, and here and there against them bloomed tall evergreen shrubs. At one upper corner of the main path was a camellia and at the other a crape-myrtle, symbols respectively, to the visitor, of Aunt Corinne and Aunt Yvonne. The brick doorstep smiled as red as the garden borders, and as he reached the open door Aline, with her two aunts at her back, received him.

"Mr. Chester—Mlle. Chapdelaine. Mr. Chester—my Aunt Yvonne." Never had the niece seemed quite so fair—in face, dress, figure, or mental poise. She wore that rose whose petals are deep red in their outer circle and pass from middle pink to central white and deepen in tints with each day's age. If that rose could have been a girl, mind, soul, and all, a Creole girl, there would have been two on one stem.

And there, on either side of her sat the aunts: the elder much too lean, the younger much too dishevelled, and both as sun-tanned as harvesters, betraying their poverty in flimsy, faded gowns which the dismayed youth named to himself not draperies but hangings. Yet they were sweet-mannered, fluent, gay, cordial, and unreserved, though fluttering, twittering, and ultra-feminine.

The room was like the pair. "Doubtlezz Aline she's told you ab-out that 'ouse. No? Ah, chère! is that possible? 'Tis an ancient relique, that 'ouse. At the present they don't build any mo' like that 'ouse is build'! You see those wall', those floor'? Every wall they are not of lath an' plazter, like to-day; they are of solid plank' of a thicknezz of two-inch'—and from Kentucky!"

The guest recognized the second-hand lumber of broken-up flatboats.

"Tha'z a genuine antique, that 'ouse! Sometime' we think we ought to egspose that 'ouse, to those tourist', admission ten cent'." [A gay laugh.]

"But tha'z only when Aline want' to compel us to buy some new dresses. And tha'z pritty appropriate, that antique 'ouse, for two sizter' themselve' pritty antique—ha, ha, ha!—as well as their anceztors."

"I fancy they're from 'way back," said Chester.

"We are granddaughter' of two émigrés of the Revolution. The other two they were decapitalize' on that gui'otine. Yet, still, ad the same time, we don't feel antique. We don't feel mo' than ten year'! And especially when we are showing those souvenir' of our in-fancy. And there is nothing we love like that."

"Aline, chère, doubtlezz Mr. Chezter will be very please' to see yo' li'l' dress of baptism! Long time befo', that was also for me, and my sizter. That has the lace and embro'derie of a hundred years aggo, that li'l' dress of baptism. Show him that! Oh, that is no trouble, that is a dil-ight! and if you are please' to enjoy that we'll show you our two doll', age' forty-three!—bride an' bri'groom. Go, you, Yvonne, fedge them."

The sister rose but lingered: "Mr. Chezter, you will egscuse if that bride an' groom don't look pritty fresh; biccause eighteen seventy-three they have not change' their clothingg!"

"Chérie," said Aline, "I think first we better read the manuscript, and then."

After a breath of hesitation—"Yes! read firs' and then. Alway' businezz biffo'!"

All went into the garden; not the part Chester had come through, but another only a trifle less pinched, at the back of the house. A few steps of straight path led them through its stiff ranks of larkspurs, carnations, and the like, to a bower of honeysuckle enclosing two rough wooden benches that faced each other across a six-by-nine goldfish pool. There they had hardly taken seats when Cupid reappeared bearing to the visitor, on a silver tray, the manuscript.

It was not opened and dived into with the fine flurry of the modern stage. Its recipient took time to praise the bower and pool, and the sisters laughed gratefully, clutched hands, and merrily called their niece "tantine." "You know, Mr. Chezter, 'tantine' tha'z 'auntie,' an' tha'z j'uz' a li'l' name of affegtion for her, biccause she takes so much mo' care of us than we of her; you see? But that bower an' that li'l' lake, my sizter an' me we construc' them both, that bower an' that li'l' lake."

Without blazoning it they would have him know they had not squandered "tantine's" hard earnings on architects and contractors.

"And we assure you that was not ladies' work. 'Twas not till weeks we achieve' that. That geniuz Aline! she was the arshetec'. And those goldfishes—like Aline—are self-su'porting! We dispose them at the apothecary, Dauphine and Toulouse Street—ha, ha, ha! Corinne, tha'z the egstent of commerce we ever been ab'e to make, eh?"

"And now," said Aline, "the story."

"Ah, yes," responded Mlle. Corinne, "at laz' the manuscrip'!" and Mlle. Yvonne echoed, with a queer guilt in her gayety:

"The manuscrip'! the myzteriouz manuscrip'!"

But there the gate bell sounded and she sprang to her feet. Cupid could answer it, but some one must be indoors to greet the caller.

"Yes, you, Yvonne," the elder sister said, and Aline added: "We'll not read till you return."

"Ah, yes, yes! Read without me!"

"No-no-no-no-no! We'll wait!"

"We'll wait, Yvonne." The sister went.

Chester smoothed out the pages, but then smilingly turned them face downward, and Aline said:

"First, Hector will tell us who's there."

Hector was Cupid. He came again, murmuring a name to Mlle. Corinne. She rose with hands clasped. "C'est M. et Mme. Rene Ducatel!"

"Well? Hector will give your excuses; you are imperatively engaged."

"Ah, chère, on Sunday evening! Tha'z an incredibility! Must you not let me go? You 'ave 'Ector."

"Ah-h! and we are here to read this momentous document to Hector?" The sparkle of amused command was enchanting to at least one besides Cupid.

Yet it did not win. "Chère, you make me tremble. Those Ducatel', they've come so far! How can we show them so li'l' civilization when they've come so far? An' me I'm convince', and Yvonne she's convince', that you an' Mr. Chezter you'll be ab'e to judge that manuscrip' better al-lone. Oh, yes! we are convince' of that, biccause, you know—I'm sorrie—we are prejudice' in its favor!"

Aline's lifted brows appealed to Chester. "Maybe hearing it," he half-heartedly said, "may correct your aunts' judgment."

The aunt shook her head in a babe's despair. "No, we've tri' that." Her smile was tearful. "Ah, chérie, you both muz' pardon. Laz' night we was both so af-raid about that, an' of a so affegtionate curio-zitie, that we was compel' to read that manuscrip' through! An' we are convince'—though tha'z not ab-out clocks, neither angels, neither lovers—yet same time tha'z a moz' marvellouz manuscrip'. Biccause, you know, tha'z a true story, that 'Holy Crozz.' Tha'z concerning an insurregtion of slave'—there in Santa Cruz. And 'a slave insurregtion,' tha'z what they ought to call it, yes!—to promote the sale. Already laz' night Yvonne she say she's convince' that in those Northron citie', where they are since lately so fon' of that subjec', there be people by dozen'—will devour that story!"

She tripped off to the house.

"Hector," said Aline, "you may sit down."

Cupid slid into the vacated seat. Chester dropped the document into his pocket.

"For what?" the girl archly inquired.

"I want to take it to my quarters and judge it there. Why shouldn't I?"

"Yes, you may do that."

"And now tell me of your father, or his father—the one Beloiseau knew—Théophile Chapdelaine."

"Both were Théophile. He knew them both."

"Then tell me of both."

"Mr. Chester, 'twould be to talk of myself!"

"I won't take it so. Tell the story purely as theirs. It must be fine. They were set, in conscience, against the conscience of their day——"

"So is Mr. Chester."

"Never mind that, either. We're in a joint commercial enterprise; we want a few good stories that will hang on one stem. Our business is business; a primrose by the river's brim—nothing more! Although"—the speaker reddened——

The girl blushed. "Mr. Chester, take away the 'although' and I'll tell the story."

"I take it away. Although——"

XX

THE CHAPDELAINES

"A yellow primrose was to him——"

Yonder in the parlor with the Ducatels, ignorant of the poet's lines as they, the two aunts—those two consciously irremovable, unadjustable, incarnated interdictions to their niece's marriage—saw the primrose, the "business," as the pair in the bower thought they saw it themselves. Were not Aline and Chester immersed in that tale of servile insurrection so destitute of angels, guiding stars, and lovers? And was not Hector with them? And are not three as truly a crowd in French as in American?

"Well, to begin," Chester urged, "your grandfather, Théophile Chapdelaine, was born in this old quarter, in such a street. Royal?"

"Yes. Nearly opposite the ladies' entrance of that Hotel St. Louis now perishing."

"Except its dome. I hear there's a movement——

"Yes, to save that. I hope 'twill succeed. To me that old dome is a monument of those two men."

"But if it comes down the home remains, opposite, where both were born, were they not?"

"Yes. Yet I'd rather the dome. We Creoles, you know, are called very conservative."

"Yet no race is more radical than the French."

"True. And we Chapdelaines have always been radical. Grandpère was, though a slaveholder."

"Oh, none of my ancestors justified slavery, yet as planters they had to own negroes."

"But the Chapdelaines were not planters. They were agents of ships. Fifty times on one page in the old Picayune, or in L'Abeille— 'For freight or passage apply to the master on board or to T. Chapdelaine & Son, agents.' Even then there were two Théophiles, and grandpapa was the son. They were wholesale agents also for French exporters of artistic china, porcelain, glass, bronze. Twice they furnished the hotel with everything of that kind; when it first opened, and when it changed hands. That's how they came to hold stock in it. Grandpapa, outdoor man of the firm, was every day in the rotunda, under that dome."

"Yes," Chester said, "it was a kind of Rialto, I know. They called it the 'Exchange,' as earlier they had called Maspero's."

"You love our small antiquities. So do I. Well, grandpapa did much business there, both of French goods and of ships; and because the hotel was the favorite of the sugar-planters its rotunda was one of the principal places for slave auctions."

"Yes, they were, I know, almost daily. The old slave-block is shown there yet, if genuine."

"Ah, genuine or not, what difference? From one that was there grandpère bought many slaves. He and his father speculated in them."

"Why! How strange! The son? your grandfather? the radical, who married—'Maud'?"

"Yes, the last slave he bought was for her."

"Why, why, why! He couldn't have met her be'—well—before the year of Lincoln's election."

"No, let me tell you. You remember 'Sidney'?"

"'Maud's' black maid? my uncle's Euonymus? Yes."

"Well, when she came to Maud, at Maud's home, in the North, she was still in agony about Mingo, who'd been recaptured. So Maud wrote South, to her aunt, who wrote back: 'Yes, he had been brought home, and at creditor's auction had been sold to a slave-trader to be resold here in New Orleans.' So then Sidney begged Maud, who by luck was coming here, to bring her here to find him."

"Brave Sidney. Brave Euonymus."

"Yes—although—her Southern mistress—I know not how legally—had sent to her her free-paper. That made it safer, I suppose, eh?"

"Yes. But—who told you all this so exactly—your grand'mère herself, or your grandpère?"

"Ah—she, no. I never saw her. And grandpère—no, he was killed before I was born."

"What?"

"Yes, all that I'll come to. This I'm telling now is from my own papa. He had it from grandpère. Grand'mère and Sidney came with friends, a gentleman and his wife, by ship from New York."

"And all put up at Hotel St. Louis?"

"Yes. From there Maud and Sidney began their search. But now, first, about that speculating in slaves: those two Théophiles, first the father, then both, hated slavery. 'Twas by nature and in everything that they were radical. Their friends knew that, even when they only said, 'Oh, you are extreme!' or 'Those Chapdelaines are extremist.' In those years from about eighteen-forty to 'sixty—"

"When the slavery question was about to blaze——"

"Yes—they voted Whig. That was the most antislavery they could vote and stay here. But under the rose they said: 'All right! extremist, yet Whig; we'll be extreme Whig of a new kind. We'll trade in slaves.'"

Chester laughed. "I begin to see," he said, and by a sidelong glance bade Aline note the rapt attention of Cupid. Her answering smile was so confidential that his heart leaped.

"I'll tell you by and by about that also," she murmured, and then resumed: "While grandpère was yet a boy his father had begun that, that slave-buying. On that auction-block he would often see a slave about to be sold much below value, or whose value might easily be increased by training to some trade. You see?—blacksmith, lady's maid, cook, hair-dresser, engine-driver, butler?"

Chester darkened. "So he made the thing pay?"

"Seem to pay. Looking so simple, so ordinary, 'twas but a mask for something else."

"But in a thing looking so ordinary had he no competitors, to make profits difficult?"

"Ah, of a kind, yes; but the men who could do that best would not do it at all. They would not have been respected."

"But T. Chapdelaine & Son were respected."

"Yes, in spite of that. Their friends said: 'Let the extremists be extreme that way.'"

"The public mind was not yet quite in flames."

"No. But—guess who helped grandpère do that."

"Why, do I know him? Castanado."

The girl shook her head.

"Who? Beloiseau?"

"Ah, you! You can guess better."

"Ovide Lan'—no, Ovide was still a slave."

"Yet more free than most free negroes. 'Twas he. He was janitor to offices in the hotel, and always making acquaintance with the slaves of the slave-mart. And when he found one who was quite of the right kind—and Ovide he's a wise judge of men, you know—he would show him to grandpère, and at the auction, if the bidding was low, grandpère would buy him—or her."

"What was one of 'quite the right kind'? One willing to buy his own freedom?"

"Ah, also to do something more; you see?"

"Yes, I see," Chester laughed; "to help others run away, wasn't it?"

"Not precisely to run, but——"

"To stow away, on those ships, h'm?" There was rapture in crossing that h'm line of intimacy. "I see it all! Ha-ha, I see it all! Well! that brings us back to 'Maud,' doesn't it—h'm?"

"Yes. They met, she and grandpère, at a ball, in the hotel. But"—Aline smiled—"that was not their first. Their first was two or three mornings before, when he, passing in Royal Street, and she—with Sidney—looking at old buildings in Conti Street——"

"Mademoiselle! That happened to them?—there?"

"Yes, to them, there." With level gaze narrator and listener regarded each other. Then they glanced at Cupid. His eyes were shining on them.

"Who is our young friend, anyhow?" asked Chester.

"Ah, I suppose you have guessed. He is the grandson of Sidney."

XXI

"And another time, on the morning just before the ball," said Aline, returning to the story, "they had seen each other again. That was at the slave-auction. That night, before the ball was over, she and grandpère understood—knew, each, from the other, why the other was at that auction; and he had promised her to find Mingo.

"Well, after weeks, Ovide helping, all at once there was Mingo, in the gang, by the block, waiting his turn to go on it. Picture that! Any time I want to shut my eyes I can see it, and I think you can do the same, h'm?"

Blessed h'm; 'twas the flower—of the Chapdelaines—humming back to the bee. Said the bee, "We'll try it there together some day, h'm?" and Cupid mutely sparkled:

"Oh, by all means! the three of us!"

The flower ignored them both. "There was the auctioneer," she said; "there were the slaves, there the crowd of bidders; between them the block, above them the beautiful dome. Very soon Mingo was on the block, and the first bid was from Sidney. She was the only one in a hurry except Mingo. He was trying to see her, but she was hiding from him behind grandpère; yet not from the auctioneer. The auctioneer stopped.

"'Who authorized you to bid here?' he asked her.

"'Nobody, sir; I's free.' She held up her paper.

"Grandpère nodded to the auctioneer.

"'Will Mr. Chapdelaine please read it out?'

"He read it out, signature and all.

"'Anybody know any one of that name?' the auctioneer asked, and grand'mère said:

"'That's my aunt. This free girl is my maid."

"'Oh, bidding for you?' he said; and grand'mere said no, the girl was bidding on her own account, with her own money.

"'What kind of money? We can't take shinplasters.' For 'twas then 'sixty-one—year of secession, you know.

"'Gold!' Sidney called out, and held it up in a black stocking, so high that every one laughed."

"Not Mingo, I fancy."

"Ah, no, nor the keeper of the gang."

"—Wonder how Mingo was behaving."

"He? he was shaking and weeping, and begging this and that of the man who held and threatened him, to keep him quiet. So then the auctioneer began to call Sidney's bid. You know how that would be: 'Gentlemen, I'm offered five hundred dollars. Cinq cent piastres, messieurs! Only five hundred for this likely boy worth all of nine! Who'll say six? Going at five hundred, what do I hear?' But he heard nothing till—'third and last call!' Then the owner of the gang nodded and the auctioneer called out, 'six hundred!'"

"And did Sidney raise it?"

"No, she wept aloud. 'Oh, my brotheh!' she cried, 'Lawd save my po' brotheh! I's los' him ag'in! I done bid my las' dollah at de fust call!'"

"And Mingo knew her voice, spied her out?"

"Yes, and holloed, 'Sidney! sisteh!' till grand-mère wept too and a man called out, 'No one bid that six hundred!' But grandpère said: 'I bid six-fifty and will tell all about this unlikely boy if his owner bids again.'

"So Mingo was sold to grandpère. 'And now,' grandpère whispered to grand-mère and her friends, 'go pack trunks for the ship as fast as you can.'"

"And they parted like that? But of course not!"

"No, only expected to. In the Gulf, at the mouth of the river, a Confederate privateer"—the narrator's voice faded out. She began to rise. Her aunts were returning.

XXII

Mademoiselle, we say, began to rise. Chester stood. Also Cupid. The aunts drew near, speaking with infantile lightness:

"Finizh' already that reading? You muz' have gallop'! Well, and what is Mr. Chezter's conclusion on that momentouz manuscrip'?"

The niece hurried to answer first: "Ah! we must not ask that so immediately. Mr. Chester concludes 'tis better for all that he study that an evening or two in his seclusion."

"And! you did not read it through together?"

"No, there was no advantage to——"

"Oh! advantage! An' you stop' in the mi'l of that momentouz souvenir of the pas'! Tha'z astonizhing that anybody could do that, an' leas' of all" [confronting Chester] "the daughter of a papa an' gran'papa with such a drama-tique bio-graphie! Mr. Chezter, to pazz the time Aline ought to 'ave tell you that bio-graphie, yes!—of our marvellouz brother an' papa. Ah, you should some day egstort that story from our too li'l' communicative girl."

"Why not to-day, for the book?"

"Oh, no-no-no-no-o! We di'n' mean that!" The sisters laughed excessively. "A young lady to put her own papa into a book—ah! im-pos-si-ble!"

They laughed on. "Even my sizter an' me, we have never let anybody egstort that, an' we don't know if Aline ever be persuade'—"

"Yes, some day I'll tell Mr. Chezter—whatever he doesn't know already."

"Ha-ha! we can be sure tha'z not much, Aline. And, Corinne, if

62

he's heard this or that, tha'z the more reason to tell him co'rec'ly. Only, my soul! not to put in the book, no!"

"Ah, no! Though as between frien', yes. And, moreover, to Mr. Chezter, yes, biccause tha'z so much abbout that Hotel St. Louis and he is so appreciative to old building'. Ah, we've notice' that incident! Tha'z the cause that we egs'ibit you our house—as a relique of the pas'—Yvonne! we are forgetting!—those souvenir' of our in-fancy—to show them! Come—all!"

Half-way to the house—"Ah, ha-ha! another subjec' of interess! See, Mr. Chezter; see coming! Marie Madeleine! She's mis' both her beloved miztress' from the house and become anxious, our beautiful cat! We name' her Marie Madeleine because her great piety! You know, tha'z the sacred truth, that she never catch' a mice on Sunday."

"Ah, neither the whole of Lent!"

In the parlor—"I really think," Chester said, "I must ask you to let me take another time for the souvenirs. I'm so eager to save this manuscript any further delay—" He said good-by.

Yet he did not hurry to his lodgings. He had had an experience too great, too rapt, to be rehearsed in his heart inside any small, mean room. All the open air and rapid transit he could get were not too much, till at lamplight he might sit down somewhere and hold himself to the manuscript.

Meantime the Chapdelaines had been but a moment alone when more visitors rang—a pair! Their feet could be seen under the gate—two male, two female—that is not a land where women have men's feet. Flattering, fluttering adventure—five callers in one afternoon! "Aline, we are becoming a public institution!" The aunts sprang here, there, and into collision; Cupid sped down the walk; Marie Madeleine stood in the door.

And who were these but the dear De l'Isles!

"No," they would not come inside. "But, Corinne, Yvonne, Aline, run, toss on hats for a trip to Spanish Fort."

One charm of that trip is that the fare is but, five cents, and the crab gumbo no dearer than in town. "Come! No-no-no, not one, but the three of you. In pure compassion on us! For, as sometimes in heaven among cherubim, we are ennuyés of each other!"

The small half-hourly electric train in Rampart Street had barely started lakeward into Canal, with the De l'Isle-Chapdelaine five aboard and the sun about to set, when Geoffry Chester entered—and stopped before monsieur, stiff with embarrassment. Nevertheless that made them a glad six, and, as each seat was for two, the two with life before them took one.

63

XXIII

The small public garden, named for an old redout on the lake shore at the mouth of Bayou St. John was filled with a yellow sunset as Chester and Aline moved after the aunts and the De l'Isles from the train into a shell walk whose artificial lights at that moment flashed on.

"So far from that," he was saying, "a story may easily be improved, clarified, beautified, by—what shall I say?—by filtering down through a second and third generation of the right tellers and hearers."

"Ah, yes! the right, yes! But——"

"And for me you're supremely the right one."

Instantly he rued his speech. Some delicate mechanism seemed to stop. Had he broken it? As one might lay a rare watch to his ear he waited, listening, while they stood looking off to where water, sky, and sun met; and presently, to his immeasurable relief, she responded:

"Grandpère was not at that time such a very young man, yet he still lived with his father. So when grand'mère and her two friends—with Sidney and Mingo—returned from the privateer to the hotel they were opposite neighbors to the Chapdelaines and almost without another friend, in a city—among a people—on fire with war. Then, pretty soon—" the fair narrator stopped and significantly smiled.

Chester twinkled. "Um-h'm," he said, "your grandpère's heart became another city on fire."

"Yes, and 'twas in that old hotel—with the war storm coming, like to-day only everything much more close and terrible, business dead, soldiers every day going to Virginia—you must make Mr. Thorndyke-Smith tell you about that—'twas in that old hotel, at a great free-gift lottery and bazaar, lasting a week, for aid of soldiers' families, and in a balcony of the grand salon, that grandpère—" the narrator ceased and smiled again.

"Proposed," Chester murmured.

The girl nodded. They sank to a bench, the world behind them, the stars above. "Grand'mére, she couldn't say yes till he'd first go to her home, almost at the Canadian line, and ask her family. She, she couldn't go; she couldn't leave Sidney and Mingo and neither could she take them. So by railroad at last he got there. But her family took so long to consent that he got back only the next year and through the fall of the city. Only by ship could he come, and not till he had begged President Lincoln himself and promised him to work with his might to return Louisiana to the Union. Well, of course, he and his father had voted against secession, weeping; yet now this was a pledge terrible to keep, and the more because, you see? what to do, and when and how to do it——"

"Were left to his own judgment and tact?"

"Oh, and honor! But anyhow he came. Doubtless, bringing the written permission of the family, he was happy. Yet to what bitternesses—can we say bitternesses in English?"

"Indeed we can," said Chester.

"To what bitternesses grandpére had to return!"

"Aline!" Mme. De l'Isle called; "à table!"

"Yes, madame. Tell me—you, Mr. Chester—to your vision, how all that must have been."

"Paint in your sketch? Let me try. Maybe only because you tell the story, but maybe rather because it's so easy to see in you a reincarnation of your grand'mére—a Creole incarnation of that young 'Maud'—what I see plainest is she. I see her here, two thousand miles from home, with but three or four friends among a quarter of a million enemies. I see her on the day the city fell, looking up and down Royal Street from a balcony of the hotel, while from the great dome a few steps behind her the Union fleet could be seen, rounding the first two river bends below the harbor, engaging a last few Confederate guns at the old battle-ground, and coming on, with the Stars and Stripes at every peak. I see her——"

"She was beautiful, you know—grand'mére."

"Yes, I see her so, looking down from that balcony, awestruck, not fearstruck, on the people who in agonies of rage and terror fled the city by pairs and families, or in armed squads and unarmed mobs swept through the streets and up and down the levee, burning, breaking, and plundering."

"But that was the worst anybody did, you know."

"Oh, yes. We never knew till to-day's war came how humane that war was. It wasn't a war in which beauty, age, and infancy were hideous perils."

"Ah, never mind about that to-day. But about grandpère and grand'mère go on. Let me see how much you can imagine correctly, h'm?"

"Please, mademoiselle, no. Time has made you—through your father's eyes—they say you have them—an eye-witness. So next you see your grandpère getting back at last, by ship—go on."

"Yes, I see that, in a harbor whose miles of wharfs without ships cried to him: 'our occupation and your fortune are gone!' Also I see him again in the streets—Royal, Chartres, Canal, Carondelet— where old friends pass him with a stare. I see him and grand'mère married at last, in a church nearly empty and even the priest unfriendly."

"Had he no new friends, Unionists?"

"Not yet, at the wedding. There he said: 'Old friends or none.' And that was right, don't you think? Later 'twas different. You see, in the navy, both of the rivers and the sea, as likewise the army, grand'mère had uncles and cousins; and when the hotel was made a military hospital she was there every day. And naturally those cousins, whether from hospital or no, would call and even bring friends. Well, of course, grandpère was, at the least, courteous! And then there was his word of honor, to Mr. Lincoln, as also his own desire, to bring the State back into the Union."

"Of course. Don't hurry, please."

"Was I hurrying? Pardon, but I'm afraid they'll be calling us again." The pair rose, but stood. "Well, when a kind of government was made of that part of the State held by the Union, and the military governor wanted both grandpère and his father to take some public offices, his father made excuse of his age and of a malady—taken from that hospital—which soon occasioned him to die."

"I've seen his tomb, in St. Louis cemetery, with its epitaph of barely two words—'Adieu, Chapdelaine.' Who supplied that? Old friends, after all?"

"A few old, a few new, and one the governor."

"Did the governor propose the words?"

"No. If I tell you you won't tell? Ovide. But grandpère he took the office. And so that put him yet more distant from old friends except just two or three who believed the same as he did."

"And our Royal Street coterie, of course."

"Ah, not those you see now; but their parents, yes. They were faithful; though sometimes, some of them, sympathizing differently. Well, and so there was grandpère working to repair a piece of the State, when at last the war finished and the reconstruction of the whole State commenced. He and Ovide were both of that State convention they mobbed in the 'July riot.' Some men were killed in that riot. Grandpère was wounded, also Ovide. Those were awful times to grand'mère, those years of the reconstruction. Grandpère he—" The girl glanced backward, then turned again, smiling. The four chaperons were going indoors without them.

"Yes," Chester said, "your grandpère I can imagine——"

"Well, go ahead; imagine, to me."

"No. No, except just enough to see him with no choice of party allegiance but between a rabble up to the elbows in robbery and an old régime red-handed with the rabble's blood."

66

"Ah, so papa told me, after grandpère was long gone, and me on his knee asking questions. 'Reconstruction, my dear child—' once he answered me, "twas like trying to drive, on the right road, a frantic horse in a rotten harness, and with the reins under his tail!' Ah, I wish you could have known him, Mr. Chester—my father!"

"I know his daughter."

"Well, I suppose—I suppose we must go in."

"With the story almost finished?"

"We'll, maybe finish inside—or—some day."

XXIV

T. CHAPDELAINE & SON

The seniors were found at a table for four.

Mme. De l'Isle explained: "But! with only four to sit down there, how was it possib' to h-ask for a tab'e for six? That wou'n' be logical!"

When the waiter offered to add a smaller table and make one snug board for six—"No," she said; "for feet and hands that be all right; but for the mind, ah! You see, Mr. Chezter, M. De l'Isle he's also precizely in the mi'l' of a moze overwhelming story of his own——"

"Hiztorical!" the aunts broke in. "Well-known! abbout old house! in the vieux carré!"

"And," madame insisted, "'twould ruin that story, to us, to commenze to hear it over, while same time 'twould ruin it to you to commenze to hear it in the mi'l'. And beside', Aline, you are doubtlezz yet in the mi'l' of your own story and—waiter! make there at that firz' window a tab'e for two, and" [to the pair] "we'll run both storie' ad the same time—if not three!"

"Like that circ'"—the aunts fell into tears of laughter. They touched each other with finger-tips, cried, "Like that circuz of Barnum!" and repeated to the De l'Isles and then to Aline, "Like that circuz of Barnum an' Bailey!"

At the table for two, as the gumbo was uncovered and Chester asked how it was made, "Ah!" said Aline, "for a veritable gumbo what you want most is enthusiasm. The enthusiasm of both my

67

aunts would not be too much. And to tell how 'tis made you'd need no less, that would be a story by itself, third ring of the circus."

"Then tell me, further, of 'grandpère'"

"And grand'mère? Yes, I must, as I learned about them on papa's knee. Mamma never saw them; they had been years gone when papa first knew her. But Sidney I knew, when she was old and had seen all those dreadful times; and, though she often would not tell me the story, she would tell me what to ask papa; you see? You would have liked to talk with Sidney about old buildings. Mr. Chester, I think it is not that in New Orleans we are so picturesque, but that all the rest of our country—in the cities—is so starved for the picturesque. Sidney would have told you that story monsieur is telling now as well as all the strange history of that old Hotel St. Louis. First, after the war it was changed back from a hospital to a hotel. I think 'twas then they called it Hotel Royal. Anyhow 'twas again very fine. Grandpère and grand'mère were often in that salon where he had first—as they say—spoken. Because, for one thing, there they met people of the outside world without the local prejudices, you know?"

"At that time bitter and vindictive?"

"Oh, ferocious! And there they met also people of the most— dignity."

"Above the average of the other hotels?"

"Well, not so—so brisk."

"Not so American?"

"Ah, you know. Well, maybe that's one reason the St. Charles, for example, continued, while the Royal did not. Anyhow the Royal—grandpère had the life habit of it and 'twas just across the street. Daily they ate there; a real economy."

"But they kept the old home."

"Yes. 'Twas furnished the same but not 'run' the same. 'Twas very difficult to keep it, even with all three stories of the servants' wing shut up, you know?—like"—a glance indicated the De l'Isles.

"But you say Hotel Royal was soon closed."

"Yes, and then, in the worst of those days, it became the capitol. There, in the most elegant hotel for the most elegant planters of the South—anyhow Southwest—sat their slaves, with white men even more abhorred, and made the laws. In that old dome, second story, they put a floor across, and there sat the Senate! Just over that auction-block where grandpère had bought Mingo."

"Where was he—Mingo?"

"Dead—of drink. Grandpère was in that government! Long

time he was senator. Mr. Chester, for that papa was proud of him, and I am proud."

The listener was proud of her pride. "I know," he said, "from my own people, that in such an attitude—as your grandfather's—there was honor a plenty for any honorable man. Ovide tells me the negroes never wanted negro supremacy. I wonder if that's so. They were often, he says, madly foolish and corrupt; yet their fundamental lawmaking was mostly good. I know the State's constitution was; it was ahead of the times."

Aline made a quick gesture: "And any of the old masters who agreed to that could help lead!"

"Mademoiselle, how could they agree to it? Some did, I know, but that's the wonder. Those that could not—who can blame them?"

"Ah! 'tis no longer a question of blame but of judgment. So papa used to say. Anyhow grandpère agreed, accepted, led; until at the last, one day, that White League—you've heard of them, how they armed and drilled and rose against that reconstruction police in a battle on the steamboat landing? Grandpère was in that. He commanded part of the reconstruction forces. And papa was there, though only thirteen. Grandpère was bayonet-wounded. They carried him away bleeding. Only at the State-house a surgeon met them, and there, under that dome, just as papa brought grand'mère and Sidney, he died." Mademoiselle ceased.

Chester waited, but she glanced to the other table. Monsieur had ended his recital. Madame and the aunts chatted merrily. Smilingly the niece's eyes came back.

"Don't stop," said Chester. "What followed—for 'Maud'—Sidney—your boy father—your little-girl aunts? Did the clock in the sky call them North again?"

"No." The speaker rose. "I'll tell you on the train; I hear it coming."

XXV

"There's a train every half-hour," Chester said.

"Yes, but the day-laborer must be home early."

On the train—"Well," the youth urged, "your grand'mère stayed in the old home, I hope, with the three children—and Sidney?"

"Only till she could sell it. But that was nearly three years, and they were hard, those three. But at last, by the help of that Royal Street coterie—who were good friends, Mr. Chester, when friends were scarce—she sold both house and furniture—what was by that time remaining—and bought that place where we are now living."

"Was there no life-insurance?"

"A little. We have the yearly interest on it still. 'Tis very small, yet a great help—to my aunts. I tell that only to say that papa would never touch it when he and my aunts—and afterward mamma— were in very narrow places."

Chester perceived another reason for the telling of it; the niece wanted to escape the credit of being the sole support of her aunts. She read his thought but ignored it.

"Papa was very old for his age," she continued. "You may see that by his being in the battle with grandpère at thirteen years. And because of that precocity he got much training of the mind—and spirit—from grandpère that usually is got much later. I think that is what my aunts mean when they tell you papa's life was dramatic. It was so, yet not in the manner they mean, the manner of grandpère's life; you understand?"

"You mean it was not melodramatic?"

"Ah! the word I wanted! Mr. Chester, when we get over being children, those of us who do, why do we try so hard to live without melodrama?"

"Oh, mademoiselle, you know well enough. You know that's what melodrama does, itself? What is it, in essence, but a struggle to rise out of itself into a higher drama, of the spirit——?"

"A divine comedy! Yes. Well, that is what my father's life seems to me."

"With tragic elements in it, of course?"

"Oh! How could it be high comedy without? But except that one battle the tragedy was not—eh—crude, like grandpère's; was not physical. Once he said to me: 'There are things in life, in the refined life, very quiet things, that are much more tragic than bloodshed or death or the defying of death.'"

"In the refined life," Chester said musingly.

"Yes! and he was refined, yet never weak. 'Strength,' he said, 'valor, truth, they are the foundations; better be dead than without them. Yet one can have them, in crude form, and still better be dead. The noble, the humane, the chaste, the beautiful, 'tis with them we build the superstructure, the temple, of life—Mr. Chester, if you knew French I could tell you that better."

"I doubt it. Go on, please, time's a-flying."

70

"Well, you see how tragic was that life! Papa saw it and said: 'It shall not be tragic alone. I will build on it a comedy higher, finer, than tragedy. That's what life is for; mine, yours, the world's,' he said to me. Mr. Chester, you can imagine how a daughter would love a father like that, and also how mamma loved him—for years—before they could marry."

"Your mother was a Creole, I suppose?"

"No, mamma was French. After grand'mère had followed grandpère—above—papa, looking up some of the once employees of T. Chapdelaine & Son, to raise the old concern back to life, arranged with them that while they should reinstitute it here he would go live in France, close to the producers of the finest goods possible. You see? And he did that many years with a kind of success; but smaller and smaller, because little by little the taste for those refinements was passing, while those department stores and all that kind of thing—you understand—h'm?"

The train stopped in Rampart Street, and when one aunt, with madame, and one with monsieur, had followed the junior pair out of the snarlings and hootings of Canal Street's automobiles and to the quiet sidewalks of the old quarter——

"Well?" said Chester, slowing down, and——

"Well," said Aline, "about mamma: ah, 'tis wonderful how they were suited to each other, those two. Almost from the first of his living there, in France, they were acquainted and much together. She was of a fine ancestry, but without fortune; everything lost in the German war, eighteen seventy. They were close neighbor to a convent very famous for its wonderful work of the needle and of the bobbin. 'Twas there she received her education. And she and papa could have married any time if he could promise to stay always there, in France. But the business couldn't assure that; and so, for years and years, you see?"

"Yes, I see."

"But then, all at once, almost in a day, mamma, she found herself an orphan, with no inheritance but poor relations and they with already too many orphans in their care. For, as my aunts say, joking, that seems to run in our family, to become orphans.

"They are very fond of joking, my aunts. And so, because to those French relations America seemed a cure for all troubles, they allowed papa to marry mamma and bring her here to live, where I was born, and where they lived many, many years so happily, because so bravely——"

"And in such refinement—of spirit?"

"Ah, yes, yes. And where we are yet inhabiting, as you

71

perceive, my aunts and me, and—as you see yonder this moment waiting us in the gate—Hector and Marie Madeleine!"

Alone with the De l'Isles in Royal Street Chester asked, "And the business—Chapdelaine & Son?"

"Ah, sinz' long time liquidate'! All tha'z rim-aining is Mme. Alexandre. Mr. Chezter, y' ought to put that! That ought to go in the book," said monsieur.

"If we could only avoid a disjointed effect."

"Dizjoin'—my dear sir! They are going to read thad book biccause the dizjointed—by curio-zity. You'll see! That Am-erican pewblic they have a passion, an insanitie, for the dizjointed!"

XXVI

The week so blissfully begun in the Chapdelaines' garden and at Spanish Fort was near its end.

The Courier des Etats-Unis had told the Royal Street coterie of mighty doings far away in Italy, of misdoings in Galicia, and of horrors on the Atlantic fouler than all its deeps can ever cleanse; but nothing was yet reported to have "tranzpired" in the vieux carré. The fortunes of "the book" seemed becalmed.

It was Saturday evening. The streets had just been lighted. Mlles. Corinne and Yvonne, dingy even by starlight, were in one of them—Conti. Now they turned into Royal, and after them turned Chester and Aline. Presently the four entered the parlor of the Castanados. Their coming made its group eleven, and all being seated Castanado rose.

After the proper compliments—"They were called," he said, "to receive——"

"And discuss," Chester put in.

"To receive and discuss the judgment of their——"

"The suggestions," Chester amended.

"The judgment and suggestion' of their counsel, how tha'z best to publish the literary treasure they've foun' and which has egspand' from one story to three or four. Biccause the one which was firzt acquire' is laztly turn' out to be the only one of a su'possible incompat'—eh—in-com-pat-a-bil-ity—to the others." His bow yielded the floor to Chester. "Remain seated, if you please," he said.

"In spite of my wish to save this manuscript all avoidable delay," Chester began, "I've kept it a week. I like it—much. I think that in quieter times, with the reading world in a more contemplative mood, any publisher would be glad to print it. At the same time it seems to me to have faults of construction that ought to come out of it before it goes to a possibly unsympathetic publisher. Yet after—was Mme. Alexandre about——?"

"Juz' to say tha'z maybe better those fault' are there. If the publisher be not sympathetique we want him to rif-use that manuscrip'."

"Yes!" several responded. "Yes! He can't have it! Tha'z the en' of that publisher."

"Well, at any rate," Chester said, "after using up this whole week trying, fruitlessly, to edit those faults out of it, here it is unaltered. I still feel them, but I have to confess that to feel them is one thing and to find them is quite another. Maybe they're only in me."

"Tha'z the only plase they are," said Dubroca, with kind gravity. "I had the same feeling—till a dream, which reveal' to me that the feeling was my fault. The manuscrip' is perfec'."

"Messieurs," Mme. Castanado broke in, "please to hear Mlle. Aline." And Aline spoke:

"Perfect or no, I think that's what we don't require to conclude. But if that manuscript will join well with those other two—or three, or four, if we find so many—or if it will rather disjoint them—'tis that we must decide; is it not, M. De l'Isle?"

"Yes, and tha'z easy. That story is going to assimilate those other' to a perfegtion! For several reason'. Firz', like those other', 'tis not figtion; 'tis true. Second, like those, 'tis a personal egsperienze told by the person egsperienzing. Third, every one of those person' were known to some of us, an' we can certify that person that he or she was of the greatez' veracity! Fourth, the United States they've juz' lately purchaze' that island where that story tranzpire. And, fifthly, the three storie' they are joint'; not stiff', like board' of a floor, but loozly, like those link' of a chain. They are jointed in the subjec' of friddom! 'Tis true, only friddom of negro', yet still— friddom! An', messieurs et mesdames, that is now the precise moment when that whole worl' is wile on that topique; friddom of citizen', friddom of nation', friddom of race', friddom of the sea'! And there is ferociouz demand for short storie' joint' on that topique, biccause now at the lazt that whole worl' is biccome furiouzly conscientiouz to get at the bottom of that topique; an' biccause those negro' are the lowez' race, they are there, of co'se, ad the bottom!"

73

"M. Beloiseau?" the chair—hostess—said; and Scipion, with languor in his voice but a burning fervor in his eye, responded:

"I think Mr. Chezter he's speaking with a too great modestie—or else dip-lomacie. Tha'z not good! If fid-elitie to art inspire me a conceitednezz as high"—his upthrown hand quivered at arm's length—"as the flagpole of Hotel St. Louis dome yonder, tha'z better than a modestie withoud that. That origin-al manuscrip' we don't want that ag-ain; we've all read that. But I think Mr. Chezter he's also maybe got that riv-ision in his pocket, an' we ought to hear, now, at ones, that riv-ision!"

Miles. Corinne and Yvonne led the applause, and presently Chester was reading:

XXVII

THE HOLY CROSS

This is a true story. Only that fact gives me the courage to tell it. It happened.

It occurred under my own eyes when they were far younger than now, on a beautiful island in the Caribbean, some twelve hundred miles southeastward from Florida, the largest of the Virgin group—the island of the Holy Cross. Its natives called it Aye-Aye. Columbus piously named it Santa Cruz and bore away a number of its people to Spain as slaves, to show them what Christians looked like in quantity and how they behaved to one another and to strangers. You can hear much about Santa Cruz from anybody in the rum-trade.

It has had many owners. As with the woman in the Sadducee's riddle, she of many husbands, seven political powers have had this mermaid as bride. Spain, the English, the Dutch, the Spaniards again, the French, the Knights of Malta, the French again, who sold her to the Guiana Company, who in 1734 passed her over to the Danes, from whom the English captured her in 1807 but restored her again at the close of Napoleon's wars. Thus, at last, Denmark prevailed as the ruling power; but English remained the speech of the people. The island is about twenty-three miles long by six wide.

Its two towns are Christiansted on the north and Fredericksted on the south. Christiansted is the capital.

In 1848 I lived in Fredericksted, on Kongensgade, or King Street, with my aunts, Marion, Anna, and Marcia, and my grandmother—whom the servants called Mi'ss Paula—and was just old enough to begin taking care of my dignity. Whether I was Danish, British, or American I hardly knew. When grandmamma, whose husband had been of a family that had furnished a signer of our Declaration, told me stories of Bunker Hill and Yorktown I glowed with American patriotism. But when she turned to English stories, heroic or momentous, she would remind me that my father and mother were born on this island under British sway, and— "Once a Briton always a Briton." And yet again, my playmates would say:

"When you were born the island was Danish; you are a subject of King Christian VIII."

Kongensgade, though narrow, was one of the main streets that ran the town's full length from northeast to southwest, and our home was a long, low cottage on the street's southern side, between it and the sea. Its grounds sloped upward from the street, widened out extensively at the rear, and then suddenly fell away in bluffs to the beach. It had been built for "Mi'ss Paula" as a bridal gift from her husband. But now, in her widowhood, his wealth was gone, and only refinement and inspiring traditions remained.

The sale or hire of her slaves might have kept her in comfort; but a clergyman, lately from England, convinced her that no Christian should hold a slave, and setting them free she accepted a life of self-help and of no little privation. She was his only convert. His zeal cooled early. Her ex-slaves, finding no public freedom in custom or law, merely hired their labor unwisely and yearly grew more worthless.

[The reader lifted his eyes across to Aline:
"I had a notion to name that much 'The Time,' and this next part 'The Scene.' What do you think?"

"Yes, I think so. 'Twould make the manner of it less antique."

"Ah!" cried Mlle. Corinne, "'tis not a movie! Tha'z the charm, that antie-quitie!"

"Yes," the niece assented again, "but even with that insertion 'tis yet as old-fashioned as 'Paul and Virginia.'"

"Or 'Rasselas,'" Chester suggested, and resumed his task.]

XXVIII

(THE SCENE)

Yet to be poor on that island did not compel a sordid narrowing of life. You would have found our living-room furnished in mahogany rich and old. In a corner where the airs came in by a great window stood a jar big enough to hide in, into which trickled a cool thread of water from a huge dripping-stone, while above these a shelf held native waterpots whose yellow and crimson surfaces were constantly pearled with dew oozing through the porous ware. On a low press near by was piled the remnant of father's library, and on the ancient sideboard were silver candlesticks, snuffers, and crystal shades.

But it was neither these things nor cherished traditions that gave the room its finest charm. It was filled with the glory of the sea. There was no need of painted pictures. Living nature hung framed in wide high windows through which drifted in the distant boom of surf on the rocks, and salt breezes perfumed with cassia.

Outside, round about, there was far more. A broad door led by a flight of stone steps to the couchlike roots of a gigantic turpentine-tree whose deep shade harbored birds of every hue. To me, sitting there, the island's old Carib name of Aye-Aye seemed the eternal consent of God to some seraph asking for this ocean pearl. All that poet or prophet had ever said of heaven became comprehensible in its daily transfigurations of light and color scintillated between wave, landscape, and cloud—its sea like unto crystal, and the trees bearing all manner of fruits. Grace and fragrance everywhere: fruits crimson, gold, and purple; fishes blue, orange, pink; shells of rose and pearl. Distant hills, clouds of sunset and dawn, sky and stream, leaf and flower, bird and butterfly, repeated the splendor, while round all palpitated the wooing rhythm of the sea's mysterious tides.

The beach! Along its landward edge the plumed palms stood sentinel, rustling to the lipping waters and to the curious note of the Thibet-trees, sounding their long dry pods like castanets in the evening breeze. By the water's margin, and in its shoals and depths, what treasures of the underworld! Here a sponge, with stem bearing five cups; there a sea-fan, large enough for a Titan's use yet delicate enough to be a mermaid's. Red-lipped shells; mystical eye-stones; shell petals heaped in rocky nooks like rose leaves; and, moving among these in grotesque leisure, crabs of a brilliance and variety to

76

tax the painter. All the rector told of a fallen world seemed but idle words when the sunset glory was too much for human vision and the young heart trembled before its ineffable suggestions.

I often rode a pony. If we turned inland our way was on a road double-lined with cocoa palms, or up some tangled dell where a silvery cascade leaped through the deep verdure. On one side the tall mahogany dropped its woody pears. On another, sand-box and calabash trees rattled their huge fruit like warring savages. Here the banyan hung its ropes and yonder the tamarind waved its feathery streamers. Here was the rubber-tree, here the breadfruit. Now and then a clump of the manchineel weighted the air with the fragrance of its poisonous apples, the banana rustled, or the bamboo tossed its graceful canes. Beside some stream we might espy black washerwomen beetling their washing. Or, reaching the summit of Blue Mountain, we might look down, eleven hundred feet, on the vast Caribbean dotted with islands, and, nearer by, on breakers curling in noble bays or foaming under rocky cliffs. Northward, the wilderness; eastward, green fields of sugar-cane paling and darkling in the breeze; southward, the wide harbor of Fredericksted, the town, and the black, red-shirted boatmen pushing about the harbor; westward, the setting sun; and presently, everywhere, the swift fall of the tropical night, with lights beginning to twinkle in the town and the boats in the roadstead to leave long wakes of phosphorescent light.

Of course nature had also her bad habits. There were sharks in the sea, and venomous things ashore, and there were the earthquake and the hurricane. Every window and door had heavy shutters armed with bars, rings, and ropes that came swiftly into use whenever between July and October the word ran through the town, "The barometer's falling." Then candles and lamps were lighted indoors, and there was happy excitement for a courageous child. I would beg hard to have a single pair of shutters held slightly open by two persons ready to shut them in a second, and so snatched glimpses of the tortured, flying clouds and writhing trees, while old Si' Myra, one of the freed slaves who never had left us, crouched in a corner and muttered:

"Lo'd sabe us! Lo'd sabe us!"

Once I saw a handsome brig which had failed to leave the harbor soon enough stagger in upon the rocks where it seemed her masts might fall into our own grounds, and grandmamma told me that thus my father, though born in the island, had first met my mother.

XXIX

(THE PLAYERS)

Si' Myra was a Congo. She believed the Obi priests could boil water without fire, and in many ways cause frightful woes. To her own myths she had added Danish ones. "De wehr-wolf, yes, me chile! Dem nights w'en de moon shine bright and de dogs a-barkin', you see twelb dogs a-talkin' togedder in a ring, and one in de middle. Dah dem wait till dem yerry [hear] him; den dem take arter him, me chile," etc.

Strangest, wildest practice of the slaves was the hideous misuse Christian masters allowed them to make of Chrismas Day and week. It was then they danced the bamboula, incessantly. All through the year this Saturnalia was prepared for in meetings held at night by their leaders. The songs to which they danced were made of white society's scandals reduced to satirical rhyme; and to the rashest girl or man there was power in the warning, "You'll get yourself sung about at Christmas." Yearly a king, queen, and retinue were elected. The dresses of court and all were a mixture of splendor and tawdriness that exhausted the savings and pilferings of a twelvemonth. Good-natured "missies" often helped make these outfits. They were of velvet, silk, satin, cotton lace, false flowers, the brilliant seeds of the licorice and coquelicot, tinsel, beads, and pinch-beck. Sometimes mistresses even lent—firmly sewed fast— their own jewelry.

On Christmas Eve, here and there in the town, ground-floor rooms were hired and decorated with palm branches; or palm booths were built, decked with oranges and boughs of cinnamon berries, lighted with candles and lanterns and furnished with seats for the king, queen, and musicians, and with buckets of rum punch. Then the "bulrush man" went his round. Covered with capes and flounces of rushes and crowned with a high waving fringe of them, he rattled pebbles in calabashes, danced to their clatter, proclaimed the feast, and begged such of us white children as his dress did not terrify, for stivers from our holiday savings.

Soon the dancers began to gather in the booths; women in gorgeous trailing gowns, the men bearing showy batons and clad in gay shirts or satin jackets, and with a mongrel infant rabble at their heels. When the goombay—a flour-barrel drum—sounded, the town knew the bamboula had begun. On two confronting lines, the men

78

in one, the women in the other, a leading couple improvised a song and all took up the refrain. The goombay beat time, and the dancers rattled or tinkled the woody seed-cases of the sand-box tree set on long handles and with each of their lobes painted a separate vivid color; rattles of basketwork; and calabashes filled with pebbles and shells. All instruments were gay with floating ribbons. So the lines approached each other by two steps, receded, advanced, and receded, always in wild cadence to the signals of voice and instrument; then bowed so low that they touched—twice—thrice; then pirouetted and resumed the first movement, and now and then, with two or three turns or bows, clashed their rattles together in time. As night darkened, the rude lights flared yellow and red upon the dusky forms bedizened with beads, bangles, and grotesquer trumpery. Faces, necks, arms reeked and shone in the heat, ribbons streamed, gross odors arose, the goombay dominated all, and children of the master race—for even I was permitted to witness these orgies—without comprehending, stood aghast. Close outside, the matchless night lay on land and sea; a relieved sense caught ethereal perfumes and was soothed by the exquisite refinement into whose space and silence the faint deep voice of the savage drum sobbed one grief and one prayer alike for slave and master.

The revel always ended with New Year's Day. The next morning broke silently, and with the rising of the sun the plantation bell or the conch called the bondman and bondwoman into the cane-fields. Then, alike in broadest noon or deepest night, a spectral fear hovered wherever the master sat among his loved ones or rode from place to place. Not often did the hand of oppression fall upon any slave with illegal violence, or he or she turn to slaughter or poison the oppressor; but the slaves were in thousands, the masters were but hundreds, the laws were cruel; the whipping-post stood among the town's best houses of commerce, justice, and worship, with the thumbscrews hard by. As to armed defense, the well-drilled and finely caparisoned volunteer "troopers" were but a handful, the Danish garrison a mere squad; the governor was mild and aged, and the two towns were the width of the island apart.

XXX

(THE RISING CURTAIN)

In that year, 1848, this unrest was much increased. King Christian had lately proclaimed a gradual emancipation of all slaves in his West Indian colonies. A squad of soldiers had marched through the streets, halting at corners and beating a drum—"beating the protocol," as it was termed—and reading the royal edict. After twelve years all slaves were to go free; their owners were to be paid for them; and meantime every infant of a slave was to be free at birth.

I suppose no one knows better than the practical statesman how disastrous measures are apt to be when designed for the gradual righting of a public evil. They rarely satisfy any class concerned. In this case the aged slaves bemoaned a promised land they might never live to enter; younger ones dreaded the superior liberty of free-born children; and the planters doubted they would be paid, even if emancipation did not bring fire, rapine, and death.

One day, along with all "West-En'," as the negroes called Fredericksted—Christiansted was "Bass-En',"—I saw two British East-Indiamen sail into the harbor. Such ships never touched at Fredericksted; what could the Britons want?

"Water," they said, "and rest"; but they stayed and stayed! their officers roaming the island, asking many questions, answering few. What they signified at last I cannot say, except that they became our refuge from the black uprising that was near at hand. Likely enough that was their only errand.

Sunday, the 2d of July, was still and fair. To me the Sabbath was always a happy day. High-stepping horses prancing up to the church-gates brought friends from the plantations. The organ pealed, the choir chanted, the rector read, and read well; the mural tablets told the virtues of the churchyard sleepers, and out through the windows I could gaze on the clouds and the hills. After church came the Sunday-school. Its house was on a breezy height where the wind swept through the room unceasingly, giving wings to the children's voices as we sang, "Now be the gospel banner."

But this Sunday promised unusual pleasure. I was to go with Aunt Marion to dine soon after midday with a Danish family, in real Danish West Indian fashion, and among the guests were to be some officers of the East-Indiamen. I carried with me one fear—that we

should have pigeon-pea soup. Whoever ate pigeon-pea soup, Si'
Myra said, would never want to leave the island, and I longed for
those ships to go. But in due time we were asked:

"Which soup will you have—guava-berry or pigeon-pea?"

Hoping to be imitated I chose the guava-berry; but without
any immediately visible effect one officer took one and another the
other. After soup came an elegant kingfish, and by and by the
famous callalou and other delicate and curious viands. For dessert
appeared "red groat"; sago jelly, that is, flavored with guavas,
crimsoned with the juice of the prickly-pear and floating in milk;
also other floating islands of guava jelly beaten with eggs. Pale-
green granadillas crowned the feast. These were eaten with sugar
and wine, and before each draft the men lifted their glasses high to
right and left and cried: "Skoal! Skoal!" As the company finally rose,
our host and hostess shook hands with all, these again saluting each
other, each two saying: "Vel be komme"—"May this feast do you
good."

There was strange contrast in store for us. Late in the
afternoon we started home. On the way two friends, a lady and her
daughter, persuaded us to turn and take a walk on the north-side
road, at the town's western border. It drew us southward toward
"the lagoon," near to where this water formed a kind of moat behind
the fort, and was spanned by a slight wooden bridge. While we went
the sun slowly sank through a golden light toward the purple sea,
among temples, towers, and altars of cloud.

As we neared this bridge two black men crossing it from
opposite ways stopped and spoke low:

"Yes, me yerry it; dem say sich t'ing' as nebber bin known
befo' goin' be done in West-En' town to-night."

"Well, you look sharp, me frien'——"

Seeing us, they parted abruptly, one troubled, the other
pleased and brisk. Our friends drew back: "What does he mean,
mother?"

"Oh, some meeting to make Christmas songs, I suppose."

"I think not," said Aunt Marion. "Let's go back; my mother's
alone."

Just then Gilbert, young son of an intimate neighbor,
appeared, saying to the four of us: "I've come to find you and see
you home. The thing's on us. The slaves rise to-night. Some free
negroes have betrayed them. At eight o'clock they, the slaves, are to
attack the town."

Our home was reached first. Grandmamma heard the news
calmly. "We're in God's hands," she said. "Gilbert, will you stop at

Mr. Kenyon's" [another neighbor] "and send Anna and Marcia home?"

Mr. Kenyon came bringing them and begging that we all go and pass the night with him. But grandmamma thought we had better stay home, and he went away to propose to the neighborhood that all the women and children be put into the fort, that the men might be the freer to defend them.

"Marion," said grandmamma, "let us have supper and prayers."

The meal was scarcely touched. Aunt Marcia put Bible and prayer-book by the lamp and barred all the front shutters. When grandmamma had read we knelt, but the prayer, was scarcely finished when Aunt Marcia was up, crying: "The signal! Hear the signal!" Out in the still night a high mournful note on a bamboo pipe was answered by a conch, and presently the alarm was ringing from point to point, from shells, pipes and horns, and now and then in the solemn clangor of plantation bells. It came first from the south, then from the east, swept around to the north, and answered from the western cliffs, springing from hilltop to hilltop, long, fierce, exultant. We stood listening and, I fear, pale. But by and by grandmamma took her easy chair.

"I will spend the night here," she said.

Aunt Anna took a rocking-chair beside her. Aunt Marcia chose the sofa. Aunt Marion spread a pallet for me, lay down at my side, and bade me not fear but sleep. And I slept.

XXXI

(REVOLT AND RIOT)

Suddenly I was broad awake. Distant but approaching, I heard horses' feet. They came from the direction of the fort. Aunt Marcia was unbarring the shutters and fastening the inner jalousies so as to look out unseen.

"It's nearly one o'clock," some one said, and I got up, wondering how the world looked at such an hour. All hearkened to the nearing sound.

"Ah!" Aunt Marcia gladly cried, "the troopers!"

There were only some fifty of them. Slowly, in a fitful moonlight, they dimly came, hoofs ringing on the narrow macadam, swords clanking, and dark plumes nodding over set faces, while the distant war-signal from shell, reed, and horn called before, around, and after them.

Still later came a knock at the door, and Mr. Kenyon was warily readmitted. He explained the passing of the troopers. They had hurried about the country for hours, assembling their families at points easy to defend and then had come to the fort for ammunition and orders; but the captain of the fort, refusing to admit them without the governor's order, urged them to go to their homes.

"But," Mr. Kenyon had interposed, "a courier can reach the governor in an hour and a half."

"One will be sent as soon as it is light," was the best answer that could be got.

Our friend, much excited, went on to tell us that the town militia were without ammunition also. He believed the fort's officers were conniving with the revolt. Presently he left us, saying he had met one of our freed servants, Jack, who would come soon to protect us. Shortly after daybreak Jack did appear and mounted guard at the front gate. "Go sleep, ole mis's. Miss Mary Ann" [Marion], "you-all go sleep. Chaw! wha' foo all you set up all night? Si' Myra, you go draw watah foo bile coffee."

The dreadful signals had ceased at last, and all lay down to rest; but I remained awake and saw through the great seaward windows the wonderful dawn of the tropics flush over sky and ocean. But presently its heavenly silence was broken by the gallop of a single horse, and a Danish orderly, heavily armed, passed the street-side windows, off at last for Christiansted.

Soon the conchs and horns began again. With them was blent now the tramp of many feet and the harsh voices of swarming insurgents. Their long silence was explained; they had been sharpening their weapons.

Their first act of violence was to break open a sugar storehouse. They mixed a barrel of sugar with one of rum, killed a hog, poured in his blood, added gunpowder, and drank the compound—to make them brave. Then with barrels of rum and sugar they changed a whole cistern of water into punch, stirring it with their sharpened hoes, dipping it out with huge sugar-boiler ladles, and drinking themselves half blind.

Jack dashed in from the gate: "Oh, Miss Marcia, go look! dem a-comin'! Gin'ral Buddoe at dem head on he w'ite hoss."

We ran to the jalousies. In the street, coming southward toward the fort, were full two thousand blacks. They walked and ran, the women with their skirts tied up in fighting trim, and all armed with hatchets, hoes, cutlasses, and sugar-cane bills. The bills were fitted on stout pole handles, and all their weapons had been ground and polished until they glittered horridly in their black hands and above the gaudy Madras turbans or bare woolly heads and bloodshot eyes.

"Dem goin' to de fote to ax foo freedom," Jack cried.

At their head rode "Gin'ral Buddoe," large, powerful, black, in a cocked hat with a long white plume. A rusty sword rattled at his horse's flank. As he came opposite my window I saw a white man, alone, step out from the house across the way and silently lift his arms to the multitude to halt.

They halted. It was the Roman Catholic priest. For a moment they gave attention, then howled, brandished their weapons, and pressed on. Aunt Marcia dropped to her knees and in tears began to pray aloud; but we cried to her that Rachel, a slave woman, was coming, who must not see our alarm. Indeed, both Rachel and Tom had already entered.

"La! Miss Mary Ann, wha' fur you cryin'? Who's goin' tech you?" Rachel held by its four corners a Madras kerchief full of sugar. "Da what we done come fur, to tell Miss Paula" [grandmamma] "not be frightened."

Tom was off again while grandmamma said: "Rachel, you've been stealing."

"Well, Miss Paula! ain't I gwine hab my sheah w'en dem knock de head' out dem hogsitt' an' tramp de sugah under dah feet an' mix a whole cisron o' punch?"

Rachel told the events of the night. But as she talked a roar without rose higher and higher, and I, running with Jack to the gate, beheld two smaller mobs coming round a near corner. The foremost was dragging along the ground by ropes a huge object, howling, striking, and hacking at it. The other was doing the same to something smaller tied to a stick of wood, and the air was full of their cries:

"To de sea! Frow it in de sea! You'll nebber hole obbe" [us] "no mo'! You'll be drownded in de sea-watah!" Their victims were the whipping-post and the thumbscrews.

Tom returned to say: "Dem done to'e up de cote-house and de Jedge's house, an' now dem goin' Bay Street too tear up de sto'es."

Gilbert came up from the fort telling what he had seen. The blacks had tried to scale the ramparts, on one another's shoulders, howling for freedom and defying the garrison to fire. But the commander had not dared without orders from the governor, and his courier had not returned. A leading merchant standing on the fort wall was less discreet: "Take the responsibility! Fire! Every white man on the island will sustain you, and you'll end the whole thing here!"

Upon that word off again up-town had gone the whole black swarm, had sacked the bold merchant's store, and seemed now, by the noises they made, to be sacking others. "I come," Gilbert said, "with an offer of the ship-captains to take the white people aboard the ships."

As he turned away groups of negroes began to dash by laden with all sorts of "prog" [booty] from the wrecked stores. Grandmamma had lain down, my aunts were trying to make up some sort of midday meal, and I was standing alone behind the jalousies, when a ferocious-looking negro rattled them with his bill.

"Lidde gal, gi' me some watah."

"Wait a minute," I said, and left the room. If I hid he might burst in and murder us. So I brought a bowl of water.

"Tankee, lidde missee," he said, returned the bowl, and went away. Tom was thereupon set to guard the gate, which he did poorly. Another negro slipped in and sat down on our steps. He looked around the pretty enclosure, gave a tired grunt, and said:

"Please, missee, lemme res'; I done bruk up." He held in his hands the works of a clock, fell to studying them, and became wholly absorbed.

Rachel asked him who had broken it. He replied:

"Obbe" [our] "Ca'lina. She no like de way it talkin'. She say: 'W'at mek you say, night und day, night und day?' Un' she tuk her bill un' bruk it up. Un' Georgina chop' up de pianneh, 'caze it wouldn' talk foo her like it talk too buckra. Da shame!"

But now came yells and cheers in the street, the rush and trample of hundreds, and the cry:

"De gub'nor! de gub'nor a-comin'!"

XXXII

(FREEDOM AND CONFLAGRATION)

We ran to the windows. In an open carriage, with two official attendants, surrounded by a mounted guard and clad in the uniform of a Danish general, the aged governor came. On his breast were the insignia of the order of Dannebrog. His cavalcade could hardly make its way, and when one of the crowd made bold to seize the horses' reins the equipage, just before our house, stopped. The governor sat still, very pale.

Suddenly he rose, uncovered, and with graceful dignity bowed. Then he unfolded a paper with large seals attached, and in a trembling but clear voice began to read. In the name and by the authority of his Majesty Christian VIII, King of Denmark, he proclaimed freedom to every slave in the Danish West Indies.

Our cries of dismay were drowned in the huzzas of the black mob: "Free! Free! God bless de gub'nor! Obbe is free!"

The retinue moved again; but the crowd, ignoring the command to disperse to their homes, surged after it in transports of rejoicing. At the fort the proclamation, with the order to disperse, was read again. But the mob, suddenly granted all its demands, could not instantly return to quiet toils made odious by slavery. Mad with joy and drink, it broke into small companies, some content to stay in town carousing, others roaming out among the island estates to pillage and burn. Here the governor, in failing to employ prompt measures of police, proved himself weak.

At evening, leaving our house in care of Jack and Tom, we went to spend the night at Mr. Kenyon's, where several neighbors were gathered, under arms. Our way led us by the ruined courthouse, where for several squares the ground was completely covered with torn records, books, and other documents.

The night wore by in fitful sleep or anxious vigils. Near us all was quiet; but the distant sky was in many places red with incendiary fires. At dawn Mr. Kenyon, Gilbert, and others ventured out, and returned with sad tidings brought by courier from Christiansted. At the signal on Sunday night the negroes had swarmed there by thousands. Next day, when the governor had just departed for our town, leaving word to do nothing in his absence, they had attacked the fort as they had ours. But its commander, of a sturdy temper, had opened fire, killing and wounding many. This had only defended the town at the expense of the country, into

86

which thousands scattered to break, pillage, and burn. Yet even so no whites had been killed except two or three men who had opposed the blacks single-handed, although the whole island, outside the two towns, was at the mercy of the insurgents.

However, there was better news. A Danish man-of-war was near by. A schooner was gone to look her up, and another to ask aid in the island of Porto Rico, only seventy miles away and heavily garrisoned with Spaniards. Still it was deemed wise to accept for Fredericksted the offer from the ships and send the women and children on board, so that the military might be free to hold the uprising in check until a stronger force could extinguish it.

"Tom," Mr. Kenyon said, "is to have a boat at the beach to take us off to an American schooner. Pack no trunks. Gather your lightest valuables in small bundles. Be quick; if a crowd gets there before you you may be refused."

We hurried home over a carpet of archives and title-deeds, swallowed a sort of breakfast, and began the hard task of choosing the little we could take from the much we must leave, in a dear home that might soon be in ashes.

On the schooner we found a kind welcome, amid a throng of friends and strangers, and a chaos of boxes, bundles, and trunks. Children were crying to go home, or viewing with babbling delight the wide roadstead dotted with boats still bringing the fugitives to every anchored vessel. Women were calling farewells and cautions to the men in the returning boats, and meeting friends were telling in many tongues the droll or sad distresses of the hour.

A friend, with his wife and little daughter, gave us a thrilling story. Except their house-keeper, a young English girl, they three were the only white persons on their beautiful "North End" estate when on Sunday night their slaves came to them in force demanding "freedom papers."

"Not under compulsion, never!"

"Den obbe set eb'ryt'ing on fiah! Wen yo' house bu'n up we try t'ink w'at too do wid you and de missie!" They rushed away to the sugar-works, yelling: "Git bagasse foo bu'n him out!"

The household loaded all the firearms in the house, filled all vessels with water, and piled blankets here and there to fight fire. Then they made merry. The wife played her piano till after midnight. Whether moved by this show or not, the blacks failed to return, and next day the family escaped to the schooner.

To grandmamma and the wife of the American consul, the oldest ladies on the vessel, was given, at nightfall, the only sofa on board. The rest dropped asleep on boxes and bundles anywhere. For my couch the boatswain lent me his locker, and for a pillow a bag of something that felt like rope ends, and for three successive mornings I was wakened with:

"Sorry to disturb you, little miss, but I must get to my locker."

XXXIII

(AUTHORITY, ORDER, PEACE)

Three days of heat, glare, hubbub, and anxious suspense dragged away, and Thursday's gorgeous sunset brought a change. The Danish frigate, bright with flags and swarming with sailors, swept in, dropped anchor, and wrapped herself in thunder and white smoke. Soon she lowered a boat, a glittering officer took its tiller-ropes, its long oars flashed, and it bore away to the fort. But evening fell, a starry silence reigned, and when a late moon rose we slept.

Next morning we knew that Captain Erminger, of the frigate, had assumed command over the whole island, declared martial law, landed his marines, and begun operations. Soon the harbor was populous again, with refugees returning home. Tom came with his boat. Just as we started landward a schooner came round the bluffs bringing the Spaniards. At early twilight these landed and marched with much clatter through the vacant streets to the town's various points of entrance, there to mount guard, the Danes having gone to scatter the insurgents.

The pursuing forces, in two bodies, were to move toward each other from opposite ends of the island, spanning it from sea to sea and meeting in the centre, thus entirely breaking up the bands of aimless pillagers into which the insurrection had already dispersed. This took but a few days. Buddoe was almost at once trapped by the baldest flatteries of two leading Danish residents and, finding himself without even the honor of armed capture, betrayed his confederates and disappeared.

Only one small band of blacks made any marked resistance. Under a certain "Moses" they occupied a hill, hurling down stones upon their assailants, but were soon captured. Many leaders of the revolt were condemned and shot, displaying in most cases a total absence of fortitude.

In less than a week from the day of flight to the ships quiet was restored, and a meeting of planters was adopting rules and rates for the employment of the freed slaves. Some estates resumed work at once; on others the ravages of the torch had first to be repaired. Some negroes would not work, and it was months before all the windmills on the hills were once more whirling. The Spaniards lingered long, but were finally relieved by a Danish regiment. Captain Erminger was commended by his home government. The governor was censured and superseded. The planters got no pay for their slaves.

The government may have argued that the ex-master should no more be paid for his slave than the ex-slave recover back pay for his labor; and that, after all, a general emancipation was only a moderate raising of wages unjustly low and uniform. Both kings and congresses will at times do the easy thing instead of the fair one and let two wrongs offset each other. Make haste, rising generations! and, as you truly honor your fathers, bring to their graves the garlandry of juster laws and kinder, purer days.

To different minds this true story will speak, no doubt, a varying counsel. Some will believe that the lovely island was saved from the agonies of a Haytian revolution only through iron suppression. To others it will appear that the old governor's rashly timorous edict was, after all, the true source of deliverance. Certainly the question remains, whether even the most sudden and ill-timed concession of rights, if only backed by energetic police action, is not a prompter, surer cure for public disorder than whole batteries of artillery without the concession of rights. I believe the most blundering effort for the prompt undoing of a grievous wrong is safer than the shrewdest or strongest effort for its continuance. Meanwhile, with what patience doth God wait for man to learn his lessons! The Holy Cross still glitters on the bosom of its crystal sea, as it shone before the Carib danced on its snowy sands, and as it will still shine when some new Columbus, as yet unborn, brings to it the Christianity of a purer day than ours.

Chester shook the pages together on his knee.

"Oh-h-h!" cried Mlle. Corinne to Yvonne, to Aline, to Mlle. Castanado, "the en'! and—where is all that abbout that beautiful cat what was the proprity of Dora? Everything abbout that cat of Dora—scratch out! Ah, Mr. Chezter! Yvonne and me, we find that the moze am-using part—that episode of the cat—that large, wonderful, mazculine cat of Dora! Ah, madame" [to the chair], "hardly Marie Madeleine is more wonderful than that—when Jack pritend to lift his li'l' miztress through the surf of the sea, how he flew at the throat of Jack, that aztonishing mazculine cat! Ah, M'sieu' Beloiseau!—and to scradge that!"

But Beloiseau was judicially calm. "Yes, I rim-ember that portion. Scientific-ally I foun' that very interezting; but, like Mr. Chezter, I thing tha'z better art that the tom-cat be elimin-ate."

"Well," said the chair, "w'at we want to settle—shall we accep' that riv-ision of Mr. Chezter, to combine it in the book—'Clock in the Sky,' 'Angel of the Lord,' 'Holy Crozz'—seem' to me that combination goin' to sell like hot cake'."

"Yes! Agcept!" came promptly from two or three.

"Any oppose'? There is not any oppose'—Seraphine—Marcel—you'll be so good to pazz those rif-reshment?"

XXXIV

"Tis gone—to the pewblisher?"

M. De l'Isle, about to enter his double gate, had paused. In his home, overhead, a clock was striking five of the tenth day after that second reading in the Castanados' parlor. The energetic inquiry was his.

A single step away, in the door of the iron-worker's shop, Beloiseau, too quick for Chester, at whose elbow he stood, replied: "Tis gone better! Tis gone to the editor—of the greatez' magazine of the worl'!"

"Bravo! Sinze how long?"

"A week," Chester said.

"Hah! and his rip-ly?"

"Hasn't come yet."

"Ah, look out, now! Look out he don' steal that! You di'n' write him: 'Wire answer'? You muz' do that! I'll pay it myseff!"

"I thought I'd wait one more day. He may have other manuscripts to consider."

"Mr. Chezter, that manuscrip' is not in a prize contess; 'tis only with itseff! You di'n' say that?"

"I—implied it—as gracefully as I could."

"Ah! graze'—the h-only way to write those fellow, tha'z with the big stick! 'Wire h-answer!'"

Beloiseau lifted a finger: "I don' think thad way. Firz' place, big stick or no, that hiztorie is sure to be accept'."

M. De l'Isle let out a roar that seemed to tear the lining from his throat: "Aw-w-w! tha'z not to compel the agceptanze; tha'z to scare them from stealing it! And to privend that, there's another thing you want to infer them: that you billong to the Louisiana Branch of the Authors' Protegtive H-union! Ah, doubtlezz you don't—billong; but all the same you can infer them!"

Beloiseau's response crowded Chester's out: "Well, they are maybe important, those stratagem'; but to me the chieve danger is if maybe that editor shou'n' have the sagacitie—artiztic—commercial—to perceive the brilliancy of thad story."

"Never mine! in any'ow two days we'll know. Scipion! The day avter those two, tha'z a pewblic holiday—everything shut!"

"Yes, well?"

"If that news come, 'accepted,' all of us we'll be so please' that we'll be compel to egsprezz that in a joy-ride! and even if 'rifused,' we'll need that joy-ride to swallow the indignation."

"Ah! but with whose mash-in', so it won't put uz in bankrup'cy?"

"With two mash-in'—the two of Thorndyke-Smith! He's offer' to borrow me those whiles he's going to be accrozz the lake. You'll drive the large, me the small."

"Hah! Tha'z a gran' scheme. At the en', dinner at Antoine', all the men chipping in! Castanado—Dubroca—me—Mr. Chezter, eh?"

"With the greatest pleasure if I'm included."

"Include'—hoh! By the laws of nature!" M. De l'Isle went on up-stairs.

"We had a dinner like that," Beloiseau said, "only withoud the joy-ride and withoud those three Mlles. Chapdelaine, juz' a few week' biffo' we make' yo' acquaintanze. That was to celebrate that great victory in France and same time the news of savety of our four boys ad the front."

Chester stood astounded. "What four boys?"

"You di'n' know abboud those? Ah, well, tha'z maybe biccause we don' speak of them biffo' those ladies Chapdelaine. An' still tha'z droll you di'n' know that, but tha'z maybe biccause each one he's think another he's tol' you, and biccause tha'z not a prettie cheerful subjec', eh? Yes, they are two son' of Dubroca and Castanado, soldier', and two of De l'Isle and me, aviateur'."

"And up to a few weeks ago they were all well?"

"Ah, not well—one wounded, one h'arm broke, one trench-fivver, but all safe, laz' account."

"Tell me more about them, Beloiseau. You know I don't easily ask personal questions. Tell me all I'm welcome to know, will you?"

"I want to do that—to tell you all; but"—M. Ducatel, next

neighbor above, was approaching—"better another time—ah, Rene, tha'z a pretty warm evening, eh?"

<h1 style="text-align:center">XXXV</h1>

For two days more the vast machinery of the United States mail swung back and forth across the continent and the oceans beyond, and in unnumbered cities and towns the letter-carriers came and went; but nothing they brought into Bienville or Royal Street bore tidings from that execrable editor in New York who in salaried ease sat "holding up" the manuscript once the impressionable Dora's, now the gentle Aline's. The holiday— "everything shut up"—had arrived. No carrier was abroad. Neither reason given for the joy-ride held good. Yet the project was well on foot. The smaller car was at the De l'Isles' lovely gates, with monsieur in the chauffeur's seat, Mme. Alexandre at his side, and Dubroca close behind her. The larger machine stood at the opposite curb, with Beloiseau for driver, and Mme. Dubroca—a very small, trim, well-coiffed woman with a dainty lorgnette—in the first seat behind him. Castanado waited in the street door at the foot of his stair, down which Mme. Castanado was coming the only way she could come.

Her crossing of the sidewalk and her elevation first to the running-board and then to a seat beside Mme. Dubroca took time and the strength of both men, yet was achieved with a dignity hardly appreciated by the street children, who covered their mouths, averted their faces, and cheered as the two cars, the smaller leading, moved off and turned from Royal Street into Conti on their way to pick up the three Chapdelaines.

For nearly two hundred years—ever since the city had had a post-office—the post-office had been not too superior to remain in the vieux carré. Now, like so many old Creole homes themselves, it was "away up" in the American quarter—or "nine-tenth'"—at Lafayette Square. On holidays any one anxious enough for his mail to go "away up yondah" between nine and ten A.M., could have it for the asking. And such a one was Chester.

He had his reward. Twice and again he read the magazine's name on the envelope as he bore it to the Camp Street front of the building, but would not open the missive. That should be her privilege and honor. He lifted his eyes from it and behold, here came the two cars! But where was she? Certainly not in the front one. There he made out, in pairs, M. De l'Isle and Mme. Alexandre. Mlle. Yvonne and M. Dubroca, M. Castanado, and Mme. De l'Isle. Then in the rear car his alarmed eye picked out Beloiseau and Mlle. Corinne, with Cupid between them; Mmes. Dubroca and Castanado, especially the latter; and then, oh, then! Behind the smaller woman a vacant seat and behind the vaster one Aline Chapdelaine.

"You've heard?" cried M. De Elsie, slowing to the curb. Chester fluttered his prize. "Click, clap!"—he was in without the stopping of a wheel and had passed the letter to Aline.

"Accepted?" asked several, while both cars resumed their speed up-town.

"We'll open it in Audubon Park," she said to Chester, and Mme. Castanado and Dubroca passed the word forward to Beloiseau and Mlle. Corinne. These soon got it to Castanado and Mme. De l'Isle.

"Not to be open' till Audubon Park," sped the word still forward till Mlle. Yvonne and Dubroca had passed it to Mme. Alexandre and M. De l'Isle.

"Ahah!" he said, as he turned Lee Circle and went spinning up St. Charles Avenue. "Not in the pewblic street, but in Audubon Park, and to the singing of bird'!"

XXXVI

Out near the riverside end of the park the two cars stopped abreast under a vast live-oak, and Aline, rising, opened the letter and read aloud:

MY DEAR MR. CHESTER:

Your manuscript, "The Holy Cross," accompanied by your letter of the — inst., is received and will have our early attention.

Very respectfully,

THE EDITOR.

All other outcries ceased half-uttered when the Chapdelaine sisters clapped hands for joy, crying:

"Agcepted! Agcepted! Ah, Aline! by that kindnezz and sag-

93

acitie of Mr. Chezter—and all the rez' of our Royal Street frien'—you are biccome the diz-ting-uish' and lucrative authorezz, Mlle. Chapdelaine!"

M. De l'Isle's wrath was too hot for his tongue, but Scipion stood waiting to speak, and Mme. Castanado beckoned attention and spoke his name.

"Messieurs et mesdames" he said, "that manuscrip' is no mo' agcept' than rij-ect'. That stadement, tha'z only to rilease those insuranze companie' and——"

"And to stop us from telegraphing!" M. De l'Isle broke in, "and to make us, ad the end, glad to get even a small price! Ah, mesdemoiselles, you don't know those razcal' like me!"

"Oh!" cried the tender Yvonne—original rescuer of Marie Madeleine from boy lynchers—"you don't have charitie! That way you make yo'seff un'appie."

"Me, I cann' think," her sister persevered, "that tha'z juz' for the insuranse. The manuscrip' is receive'? Well! 'ow can you receive something if you don't agcept it? And 'ow can you agcep' that if you don' receive it? Ah-h-h!"

"No," Beloiseau rejoined, "tha'z only to signify that the editorial decision—tha'z not decide'."

Mlle. Corinne lifted both hands to the entire jury: "Oh, frien', I assure you, that manuscrip' is agcept'. And tha'z the proof; that both Yvonne and me we've had a presentiment of that already sinze the biggening! Ah-h-h!"

Castanado intervened: "Mademoiselle, that lady yonder"—he gave his wife a courtier's bow—"will tell you a differenze. Once on a time she receive' a h-offer of marriage; but 'twas not till after many days thad she agcept' it." [Applause.] "But ad the en', I su'pose tha'z for Mr. Chezter, our legal counsel, to conclude."

Mr. Chester "thought that although receipt did not imply acceptance the tardiness of this letter did argue a probability that the manuscript had successfully passed some sort of preliminary reading—or readings—and now awaited only the verdict of the editor-in-chief."

"Or," ventured Mme. Alexandre, "of that editorial board all together."

M. De l'Isle shook his head and then a stiff finger: "I tell you! They are sicretly inquiring Thorndyke-Smith—lit'ry magnet—to fine out if we are truz'-worthy! And tha'z the miztake we did—-not sen'ing the photograph of Mlle. Aline ad the biggening. But tha'z not yet too late; we can wire them from firz' drug-store, 'Suspen' judgment! Portrait of authorezz coming!'"

94

All eyes, even Cupid's, turned to her. She was shaking her head. "No," she responded, with a smile as lovely, to Chester's fancy, as it was final; as final, to the two aunts' conviction, as it was lovely.

"No photograph would be convincing," Chester began to plead, but stopped for the aunts.

"Oh, impossible!" they cried. "That wou'n' be de-corouz!"

"Ladies an' gentlemen," said M. Castanado, "we are on a joy-ride."

"An' we 'ave reason!" his wife exclaimed.

"Biccause hope!" Mme. Alexandre put in.

"Yes!" said Dubroca. "That manuscrip' is not allone receive'; sinze more than a week 'tis rittain', whiles they dillib-rate; and the chateau what dillib-rate'—you know, eh? M'sieu' De l'Isle, I move you we go h-on."

They went, the De l'Isle car and then Scipion's, back to St. Charles Avenue, and turned again up-town. On the rearmost seat—

"Why so silent?" Aline inquired of Chester.

"Because so content," he said, "except when I think of the book."

"The half-book?"

"Exactly. We've only half enough stories yet.

"Though with the vieux carré full of them?"

"Oh! mostly so raw, so bald, so thin!"

"Ah, I knew you would see that. As though human life and character were—what would say?"

"I'd say crustacean; their anatomy all on the surface. Such stories are not life, life in the round; they're only paper silhouettes— of the real life's poorest facts and moments. I state the thought poorly but you get it, don't you?"

The girl sparkled, not so much for the thought as for their fellowship in it. "Once I heard mamma say to my aunts: 'So many of these vieux carré stories are but pretty pebbles—a quadroon and a duel, a quadroon and a duel—always the same two peas in the baby's rattle.'"

"There are better stories for a little deeper search," Chester said.

"Ah, she said that too! 'And not,' she said, 'because the vieux carré is unlike, but so like the rest of the world.'"

Thus they spoke, happily—even a bit recklessly—conscious that they were themselves a beautiful story without the flash of a sword or the cloud of a misdeed in range of their sight, and not because the vieux carré was unlike, but so like the rest of the world.

"Where are we going?" Aline inquired, and tried to look forward around Mme. Castanado.

"You and I," Chester said, "are going back to your father's story. You said, the other day, his life was quiet, richer within than without."

"Yes. Ah, yes; so that while of the inside I cannot tell half, of the outside there is almost nothing to tell."

"All the same, tell it. Were not he and these Royal Street men boys together?"

"Yes, though with M. De l'Isle the oldest, and though papa was away from them many years, over there in France. Yes, they were all his friends, as their fathers had been of grandpère. And they'll all tell you the same thing; that he was their hero, while at the same time that his story is destitute of the theatrical. Just he himself, he and mamma—they are the whole story."

"A sea without a wave?"

"Ah, no; yet without a storm. And, Mr. Chester, I think a sea without a storm can be just as deep as with, h'm?"

XXXVII

"Well, they married, your father and mother, over there where her people are fighting the Germans right now, and came and lived in Bourbon Street with your aunts, eh?"

"Yes, or rather my aunts with them, they were of so much more strong natures than my aunts—more strong and large while just as sweet, and that's saying much, you know."

"I see it is."

"Mr. Chester, what you see, I think, is that my aunts are perhaps the two most—well—unworldly women you ever knew."

"True. In that quality they're childlike."

"Yes, and because they are so childlike in—above all—the freedom of their speech, what I want to say of them, just this one time, is the more to their honor: that in my whole life I've never heard them speak one word against anybody."

"Not even Cupid?"

"Ah-h-h! that's a cruel joke, and false! That true Cupid, he's an assassin; while that child, he's faultless?"

The speaker really said "fauklezz," and it was a joy to Chester to hear her at last fall unwittingly into a Creole accent. "Well,

96

anyhow," he led on, "the four lived together; and if I guess right your mother became, to all this joy-ride company, as much their heroine as your father was their hero."

"'Tis true!"

"But your father's coming back from France—it couldn't save the business?"

"Alas, no! Even together, he and mamma—and you know what a strong businezz partner a French wife can be—they could not save it. Both of them were, I think, more artist than merchant, and when all that kind of businezz began to be divorce' from art and married to machinery"—the narrator made a sad gesture.

"Kultur against culture, was it? and your father not the sort to change masters."

"True again. But tha'z not all; hardly was it half. One thing beside was the miz-conduct of an agent, the man who lately"—a silent smile.

"What?—sold your aunts that manuscript?"

"Yes. But he didn' count the most. Oh, the whole businezz, except papa's, became, as we say—give me the word!"

"Americanized?"

"No, papa he always refused to call it that. Mr. Chester, he used to say that those two marvellouz blessings, machinery, democracy, they are in one thing too much alike; they are, at first— say it, you."

"Vulgarizing?"

"Yes. I suppose that has to be—at the first, h'm? And with the buying world every day more and more in love with machine work— and seeming itself to become machine work, while at the same time Americanized, papa was like a river town"—another gesture—"left by the river!"

"Yet he never went into bankruptcy? You can point with pride to that, mademoiselle."

"Ah, Mr. Chester, pride! Once I pointed, and papa—'My daughter, there are many ways to go bankrupt worse than in money, and to have gone bankrupt in none of them—' there he stopped; he was too noble for pride. No, the businezz, juz' year after year it starved to death. In the early days grandpére had two big stores, back to back; whole-sale, Chartres Street; retail, Royal, where now all that is left of it is the shop of Mme. Alexandre. Both her husband and she were with papa in the retail store, until it diminish' that he couldn' keep them, and—in the time of President Roosevelt—some New York men they bought him out. Because a new head of the custom-house, old Creole friend of papa, without solicitation except maybe of M. Beloiseau and those, appointed him superintendent of customs warehouses, you know? where they keep all kind of imported goods, so they needn't pay the tariff till they take them out to sell them in the store? h'm?"

"Yes. And he kept that place—how long?"

"Always, till he passed, he and mamma; mamma first, he two years avter. Ad the last he said to me—we chanced to be talking in Englizh—'I've lived the quiet life. If I must go I can go quietly.'

"'And still,' I said, 'if your life had been as stormy as grandpére's you'd have been always for the right, and ad the last content, I think.'

"'Yes,' he said, 'I believe I never ran away from a storm, while ad the same time I never ran avter one.' And then he said something I wrote down the same night in the fear I might sometime partly forget it."

"Have you it with you, now, here?" She showed a bit of paper, holding it low for him to read as she retained it:

On the side of the right all the storms of life—all the storms of the world—are for the perfection of the quiet life—the active-quiet life—to build it stronger, wider, finer, higher, than is possible for the stormy life to be. Whether for each man or for the nations, the stormy life is but the means; the active-quiet life, without decay of character in man or nation but with growth forever—that is the end.

The pair exchanged a look. "Thank you," murmured Chester, and presently added: "So you were left with your two aunts. Then what?"

"I'll tell you. But"—-the Creole accent faded out—"we must not disappoint the De l'Isles, nor those others, we must——"

"I see; we must notice where we're going and give and take our share of the joy."

"We mustn't be as if reading the morning paper, h'm? I think 'tis for you they've come this way instead of going on those smooth shell-roads between the city and the lake." The two cars had come up through old "Carrollton," where the Mississippi, sweeping down from Nine-Mile Point, had been gnawing inland for something like a century, in spite of all man's engineering could pile against it, and now were out on the levee road and half round the bend above.

To press her policy, "See!" exclaimed Aline, as a light swell of the ground brought to view a dazzling sweep of the river, close beyond the levee's crown and almost on a level with the eye. They were in a region of wide, highly kept sugar-plantations. Whatever charms belong to the rural life of the Louisiana Delta were at their amplest on every side. Groves of live-oak, pecan, magnolia, and

98

orange about large motherly dwellings of the Creole colonial type moved Aline to turn the conversation upon country life in Chester's State, and constrain him to tell of his own past and kindred. So time and the river's great windings slipped by with the De l'Isles undisappointed, and early in the afternoon the company lunched in the two cars, under a homestead grove. Its master and mistress, old friends of all but Chester, came running, followed by maids with gifts of milk and honey. They climbed in among the company; shared, lightly, their bread and wine; heard with momentary interest the latest news of the great war; spoke English and French in alternating clauses; inquired after the coterie's four young heroes at the French front, but only by stealth and out of Aline's hearing; and cried to Cupid, "'Ello, 'Ector! comment ça va-t-il? And 'ow she is, yonder at 'ome, that Marie Madeleine?"

Cupid smiled to his ears, but it was the absentee's two mistresses who answered for her, volubly, tenderly: "We was going to bring her, but juz' at the lazt she discide' she di'n' want to come. You know, tha'z beautiful, sometime', her capriciouznezz!"

Indoors, outdoors, the visitors spent an hour seeing the place and hearing its history all the way back to early colonial days. Then, in the two cars once more, with seats much changed about, yet with Aline and Chester still paired, though at the rear of the forward car, they glided cityward. At Carrollton they turned toward the New Canal, and at West End took the lake shore eastward—but what matter their way? Joy was with ten of them, and bliss with two—three, counting Cupid—and it was only by dutiful effort that the blissful ones kept themselves aware of the world about them while Aline's story ran gently on. It had run for some time when a query from Chester evoked the reply:

"No, 'twas easier to bear, I think, because I had not more time and less work."

"What was your work, mademoiselle? what is it now? Incidentally you keep books, but mainly you do—what?"

"Mainly—I'll tell you. Papa, you know, he was, like grandpère, a true connoisseur of all those things that belong to the arts of beautiful living. Like grandpère he had that perception by three ways—occupation, education, talent. And he had it so abboundingly because he had also the art—of that beautiful life, h'm?"

"The art beyond the arts," suggested the listener; "their underlying philosophy."

The narrator glowed. Then, grave again, she said: "Mr. Chezter, I'll tell you something. To you 'twill seem very small, but to me 'tis large. It muz' have been because of both together, those arts

99

and that art, that, although papa he was always of a strong enthusiasm and strong indignation, yet never in my life did I hear him—egcept in play—speak an exaggeration. 'Sieur Beloiseau he will tell you that—while ad the same time papa he never rebuke' that in anybody else—egcept, of course—his daughter."

"But I ask about you, your work."

"Ah! and I'm telling you. Mamma she had the same connoisseur talent as papa, and even amongs' that people where she was raise', and under the shadow, as you would say, of that convent so famouz for all those weavings, laces, tapestries, embro'deries, she was thought to be wonderful with the needle."

Chester interrupted elatedly: "I see what you're coming to. You, yourself, were born needle in hand—the embroidery-needle."

"Well, ad the least I can't rimember when I learned it. 'Twas always as if I couldn' live without it. But it was not the needle alone, nor embro'deries alone, nor alone the critical eye. Papa he had, pardly from grand-père, pardly brought from France, a separate librarie abbout all those arts, and I think before I was five years I knew every picture in those books, and before ten every page. And always papa and mamma they were teaching me from those books— they couldn' he'p it! I was very naughty aboud that. I would bring them the books and if they didn' teach me I would weep. I think I wasn' ever so naughty aboud anything else. But in the en', with the businezz always diclining, that turn' out fortunate. By and by mamma she persuade' papa to let her take a part in the pursuanze of the businezz. But she did that all out of sight of the public——"

"Had you never a brother or sister?"

"Yes, long ago. We'll not speak of that. A sizter, two brothers; but—scarlet-fever——"

The story did not pause, yet while it pressed on, its hearers musing lingered behind. Why were the long lost ones not to be spoken of? For fear of betraying some blame of the childlike aunts for the scarlet-fever? The unworthy thought was put aside and the hearer's attention readjusted.

"Even mamma," the girl was saying, "she didn' escape that contagion, and by reason of that she was compelled to let papa put me in her place in the businezz; and after getting well she never was the same and I rittained the place till a year avter, when she pas' away, and I have it yet."

"And who filled M. Alexandre's place?"

"Oh, that? Tis fil' partly by Mme. Alexandre and partly by that diminishing of the businezz—till the largez' part of it is ripairing—of old laces, embro'deries, and so forth. Madame's shop is the chief

100

place in the city for that. Of that we have all we can do. 'Tis a beautiful work.

"So tha'z all I have to tell, Mr. Chezter; and I've enjoyed to tell you that so you can see why we are so content and happy, my aunts and I—and Hector—and Marie Madeleine. H'm?"

"That's all you have to tell?"

"That is all." "But not all there is to tell, even of the past, mademoiselle."

"Ah! and why not?"

"Oh, impossible!" Chester softly laughed and had almost repeated the word when the girl blushed; whereupon he did the same. For he seemed all at once to have spoiled the whole heavenly day, until she smilingly restored it by saying:

"Oh, yes! One thing I was forgetting. Just for the laugh I'll tell you that. You know, even in a life as quiet as mine, sometimes many things happening together, or even a few, will make you see bats instead of birds, eh?"

"I know, and mistake feelings for facts. I've done it often, in a moderate way."

"Yes? Me the same. But very badly, so that the sky seemed falling in, only once."

Chester thought that if the two aunts, just then telling the biography of their dolls, were his, his sky would have fallen in at least weekly. "Tell me of that once," he said, and, knowing not why, called to mind those four soldiers in France, to her, for some reason, unmentionable.

"Well, first I'll say that the archbishop he had been the true friend of papa, but now this time, this 'once' when my sky seemed falling, both mamma and papa they were already gone. I don't need to tell you what the trouble was about, because it never happened; it only threatened to happen. So when I saw there was only me to prevent it and to——"

"To hold the sky up?"

"Yes, seeing that, it seemed to me the best friend to go to was the archbishop.

"'Well, my old and dear friend's daughter,' he said, 'what is it?'

"'Most reverend father in God, 'tis my wish to become a nun.'

"'My child, that is a beautiful sentiment.'

"'But 'tis more; even more than my wish; 'tis my resolution. I must do that. 'Tis as if I heard that call from heaven to me, Aline Chapdelaine!'

"'Ah, but that's not only your name. Your mamma, up yonder, she's also Aline Chapdelaine.'

101

"'Yes, but I know that call is to me. Ah, your Grace, surely, surely, you will not forbid me?'

"'No, my daughter. Yet at the same time that is not a thing to be done suddenly, or in desperation. I'll appoint you a season for reflection and prayer, and after that if your resolution remains the same you shall become a nun.'

"'But, for the sake of others, will not that season be made short?'

"'For your own sake, my daughter, as well as for others, I'll make it the shortest possible. Let me see; I was going to say forty but I'll make it only thirty-nine.'

"'Ah, your Grace, but in thirty-nine days——'

"He stopped me: 'Not days, my child; years.' What he said after, 'tis no matter now; pretty soon I was kneeling and receiving his benediction."

"And the sky didn't fall?"

"No, but—I can't explain to you—'twas that very visit prevent' it falling."

XXXVIII

It was in keeping with the coterie's spiritual make-up that they should know a restaurant in the vieux carré, which "that pewblic" knew not, and whose best merits were not music and fresco, but serenity, hospitality, and cuisine—-a haven not yet "Ammericanize'."

Where it was they never told a philistine. The elect they informed under the voice, as one might betray a bird's nest. It was but a step from the crumbling Hotel St. Louis, and but another or so from the spires of St. Louis Cathedral.

In it, at a round table, the joy-riders had passed the evening of their holiday. As the cathedral clock struck nine they rose to part. At the board Chester had sat next the same joy-mate allowed him all day in the car. But with how reduced a share of her attention! Half of his own he had had to give, at his other elbow, to her aunt Yvonne; half of Aline's had gone to Dubroca. The other half into half of his was but half a half and that had to be halved by a quarter

102

coming from the two nearest across the table, one of whom was Mlle. Corinne, whose queries always required thought.

"Mr. Chezter," she said, when the purchase of an evening paper had made the great over-seas strife the general theme, "can you egsplain me why they don' stop that war, when 'tis calculate' to projuce so much hard feeling?"

Explaining as best he could without previous research, Chester had turned again to Mlle. Yvonne to let her finish telling—inspire'd by an incoming course of the menu—of those happy childhood days when she and her sister and the unfortunate gentleman from whom they had bought Aline's manuscript went crayfishing in Elysian Fields street canal, always taking the dolls along, "so not to leave them lonesome"; how the dolls had visibly enjoyed the capture of each crayfish; and how she and Corinne and the dolls would delight in the same sport to-day, but, alas! "that can-al was fil' op! and tha'z another thing calculate' to projuce hard feeling."

Through such riddles and reminiscences and his replies thereto persistently ran Chester's uneasy question to himself: Why had Aline told him that story of unnamable trouble which had goaded her to seek the cloister? Why if not to warn him away from a sentiment which was growing in him like a balloon and straining his heart-strings to hold it to its proper moorings?

Now the two cars let out their passengers at the De l'Isle gates and at the door of the Castanados. Madame of the latter name, with her spouse heaving under one arm and Chester under the other, while Mme. Alexandre pushed behind, was lifted to her parlor. Returning to the street, Chester found the motors gone, MM. De l'Isle and Beloiseau gone with them, and only the two Dubrocas, the three Chapdelaines, and Cupid awaiting him.

And now, with Cupid leading, and sleeping as he led, and with a Dubroca beside each aunt, and Aline and Chester following, this remnant of the company approached the Conti Street corner, on the way to the Chapdelaine home. At the turn——

"Mademoiselle," Chester asked in a desperation too much like hers before the arch-bishop, "do you notice that, as the old hymn says, we are treading where the saints have trod? Your saints?"

"My—ah, yes, 'tis true. 'Tis here grand'mère——

"Turned that corner in her life where your grandpère first saw her. Al'—Aline."

"Mr. Chester?"

"I want this corner, from the day I first saw you turn it, to be all that to you and me. Shall it not?"

103

She said nothing. Priceless moments glided by, each a dancing ghost. Just there ahead in the dark was Bourbon Street, and a short way down among its huddled shadows were her board fence and batten gate. It was senseless to have taken this chance on so poor a margin of time, but what's done's done! "Oh, Aline Chapdelaine, say it shall be! Say it, Aline, say it!"

"Mr. Chester, it is impossible! Impossible!"

"It is not! It's the only right thing! It shall be, Aline, it shall be!"

"No, Mr. Chester, 'tis impossible. You must not ask me why, but 'tis impossible!"

"It isn't! Aline, and I ask no why. I see the trouble. It's your aunts. Why, I'll take them with you, of course! I'll take them into my care and love as you have them in yours, and keep them there while they and I live. I can do it, I've got the wherewithal! Things have happened to me fast since I first saw you turn that corner behind us. I've inherited property, and only yesterday I was taken into one of the best law firms in the city. I'll prove all that to you and your aunts to-morrow. Aline, unspeakable treasure, you shall not live the buried-alive life in which you are trying to believe yourself rightly placed and happy, my saint! My—adored—saint!"

"Yes, I must. What you ask is impossible."

XXXIX

Long after midnight Chester had not returned to his room. He could not tolerate the confinement even of the narrow streets round about it.

Far out Esplanade Avenue, uncompanioned, he was walking mile after mile beside a belt line of trolley-cars, or more than one, while at home, in Bourbon Street, Cupid slept.

But now the child awoke, startled. Four small feet were on one of his arms, and Marie Madeleine was purring, at the top of her purr, in his ear. Drowsily he crowded her away. Purring on, she slowly walked across his stomach and dropped to the floor. But soon she leaped up again to that sensitive region and purred into his nose, not at all as if to claim attention, but as though lost in thought. When he pushed her aside she dropped again to the floor, with such a quadruple thump that he looked after her, and as she loitered across his view with tail as straight up as Cleopatra's Needle, he observed just beyond her a condition of affairs that appalled him.

Cold from his small fingers and toes to his ample heart, he rose, stole into the next room, and stood by the bed where lay Mlles. Corinne and Yvonne as they had lain every night since their earliest childhood.

"Ah! oh! h'nn!" Mlle. Corinne sprang to an elbow, nervously whispering: "What is it?"

"My back do'," he murmured, "stan'in' opem."

"Oh, little boy, no, it cannot be! I bolt' it laz' evening when you was praying. You know?"

"Yass'm, but it opem now; Marie Madeleine dess gone out thu it."

Mlle. Yvonne sprang up dishevelled beside her dishevelled sister: "Mon dieu! where is Aline?"

Colder than ever in hands and feet, the wee grandson of the intrepid Sidney responded: "Stay still tell I go see."

"Yes!" whispered Mlle. Corinne, slipping to the floor and tenderly pushing him, "go! safest for everybody! And if you see a burglar don' threaten him!"

"No'm, I won't."

"No, but juz' run quick out the back door and fron' gate and holla 'fire'! Go!"

At the crack of the door she listened after him while her sister crowded close, whispering: "Ah, pauvre Aline, always wise! Like us, silent! And tha'z after all the bravezt!"

In a moment Cupid was back, less frozen yet trembling: "She am' dah. Seem' like 'tis her leave de do' opem."

"Her clothes—they are gone?"

"No'm, all dah 'cep' de cloak she tuck on de machine. Reckon she out in de honey-sucker bower whah dey sot together Sunday evenin'. Reckon Marie Madeleine gone dah. I'll go see."

"Ah, fearlezz boy, yes! Make quick!"

This time both women pushed, single file, all the way to the garden door. There they strained their sight down the path, beyond him, but the bower was quite dark. "Corinne, chére, ought not one of us to go, yo'seff?—to spare her feelings—from that li'l' negro? You don' think one of us ought to go, yo'seff?"

"No, to sen' him, that is to spare those feel'—listen! . . . Ah, Yvonne, grâce au ciel, she's there!"

They frankly wept. "Thangg the good God!"

"Yvonne, chère, you know, we are the cause of this. 'Tis

biccause juz'—you and me. And she's gone yonder juz' for one thing; to be as far from her misére as she can."

"Yes, chère, I billieve that. I think even, she muz' not see us when she's riturning." No footfall sounded, but the cat came in, tail up, purring. Back in their chamber, with wet cheeks on its unlatched door, the sisters listened.

"I know what we muz' do, Yvonne, as soon as to-morrow. Tha'z strange I never saw that biffo'!"

Cupid came and was let in. "She was al-lone, of co'se?" the pair asked from the edge of their bed.

"Oh, yass'm, o' co'se; in a manneh, yass'm."

"Mon dieu! li'l boy. In a manner? But how in a manner? Al-lone is al-lone! What she was doing?"

"Is I got to tell dat?"

"Ah, 'tit garçon! Have you not got to tell it?"

"Well, she 'uz—she 'uz prayin'."

"And tha'z the manner she was not al-lone?"

"Yas'm, dass all." The little fellow dropped to his knees, clutched a knee of either questioner, and wept and sobbed.

XL

M. Beloiseau reached across his workbench and hung up his hammer and tongs. The varied notes of two or three remote steam-whistles told him that the hour, of the day after the holiday, was five.

He glanced behind him, through his shop to the street door, where some one paused awaiting his welcome. He thought of Chester but it was Landry, with an old broad book under his elbow.

"Ah, come in, Ovide."

As he laid aside his apron he handed the visitor the piece of metal he had been making beautiful, and waved him to the drawing whose lines it was taking.

"But those whistles," the bookman said, "they stop the handworkman too."

"Yes. In the days of my father, the days of handwork, they meant only steamboat', coming, going; but now swarm' of men and

106

women, boys, and girl', coming, going, living by machinery the machine-made life."

"'Sieur Beloiseau," Landry good-naturedly, said, "you're too just to condemn a gift of the good God for the misuse men make of it."

Scipion glared and smiled at the same time: "Then let that gift of the good God be not so hideouzly misuse'."

But Ovide amiably persisted: "Without machinery—plenty of it—I should not have this book for you, nor I, nor you, ever have been born."

Chester, entering, found Beloiseau looking eagerly into the volume. "All the same, Landry," the newcomer said, "you're no more a machine product than Mr. Beloiseau himself."

The bookman smiled his thanks while he followed the craftsman's scrutiny of the pages. "'Tis what you want?" he asked, and Chester saw that it was full of designs of ironwork, French and Spanish.

Scipion beamed: "Ah, you've foun' me that at the lazt, and just when I'm wanting it furiouzly."

"Mr. Beloiseau," said Chester, "has a beautiful commission from the new Pan-American Steamship Company."

"Thanks to Mr. Chezter," said Beloiseau, "who got me the job. Hence for this book spot cash." He turned aside to a locked closet and drawer.

"You had a pleasant holiday yesterday," said Landry to Chester.

"Who told you?"

"Mesdemoiselles, the two sisters Chapdelaine. I chanced to meet them just now at the house of the archbishop, on the steps, they coming out, I going in. I had a book also for him."

"Why! What's taking them to the archbishop?" Chester put away a frown: "Did they reflect the pleasure of the holiday?"

"Mr. Chester, no." There was an exchange of gazes, but Scipion returned, counting and tendering the price of the book.

"Well, good evening," Landry said, willing to linger; but "good evening," said both the others.

Chester turned: "Beloiseau, I want to talk with you. Go, give yourself a dip, brush some of that hair, and we'll dine alone in some place away from things."

"A dip, hah! Always I scrub me any'ow till I come to the skin. Also I'll put a clean shirt. You can wait? I'll leave you this book."

Chester waited. When presently, with Scipion still picturesque though clean-shirted, they left the shop together, he gave the book a word of praise that set its owner off on the history of his craft. "But hammered into a matrix"—he drew his watch and halted: "Spanish Fort, juzt too late; half-hour till negs train; I'll show you an example, my father's work." They turned back.

Thus they lost a second train, and dined in the same snug nook as on the day before with Aline and the rest. At twilight they took seats in Jackson Square on a cast-iron bench "hardly worthy of the place," as Chester suggested.

And Scipion flashed back: "Or, my dear sir, of any worthy place! But you was asking me——"

"About those four boys over in France, one of them yours."

"Biccause sinze all day yesterday——?"

"That's it. I can't help thinking that mademoiselle is somehow the cause of their going."

"Ah, of three she is, but of my son, no. My son he was already there when that war commence', and the cause of that was a very simple and or-din-ary in him, but not in the story of my father. I would like to tell you ab-out that biccause tha'z also ab-out that house where we was juz' seeing all that open-work on those balconie', and biccause so interested, you, in old building', you are bound to hear ab-out that some day and probably hear it wrong."

"Let's have it now; she told me yesterday to ask you for it."

XLI

THE LOST FORTUNE

"Mighty solid," the ironworker said, "that old house, so square and high. They are no Creole brick it is make with, that old house."

Chester began to speak approvingly of the wide balconies running unbrokenly around its four sides at both upper stories, but Beloiseau shook his head: "They don't billong to the firz' building of that house, else they might have been Spanish, like here on the Cabildo and that old Café Veau-qui-tête. They would not be cast iron and of that complicate' disign, hah! But they are not even a French cast iron, like those and those"—he waved right and left to the wide balconies of the Pontalba buildings flanking the square with such graceful dignity. "Oh, they make that old house look pretty good, those balconie', but tha'z a pity they were not wrought iron, biccause M. Lefevre—he was rich—sugar-planter—could have what he choose, and she was a very fashionable, his ladie. They tell some strange stories ab-out them and that 'ouse; cruelty to slave', intrigue with slave', duel' ab-out slave'. Maybe tha'z biccause those iron bar' up and down in sidewalk window', old Spanish fashion; maybe biccause in confusion with that Haunted House in Royal Street, they are so allike, those two house'. But they are cock-an'-bull, those tale'. Wha's true they don' tell, biccause they don' know, and tha'z what I'm telling you ad the present.

"When my father he was yet a boy, fo'teen, fiv'teen, those Lefevre' they rent' to the grand-mère of both Castanado and Dubroca, turn ab-out, a li'l' slave girl so near white you coul'n' see she's black! You coul'n' even suspec' that, only seeing she's rent', that way, and knowing that once in a while, those time, that whitenezz coul'n' be av-void'. Myseff, me, I've seen a man, ex-slave, so white you woul'n' think till they tell you; but then you'd see it—black! But that li'l' girl of seven year', nobody coul'n' see that even avter told. Some people said: 'Tha'z biccause she's so young; when she's grow' up you'll see. And some say, 'When she get chil'ren they'll show it, those chil'ren—an' some be even dark!'

"Any'ow some said she's child of monsieur, and madame want to keep her out of sight that beneficent way. They would bet you any money if you go on his plantation you find her slave mother by the likenezz. She di'n' look like him but they insist' that also come later. Any'ow she's rent' half-an'-half by those grand-mère' of Castanado and Dubroca, at the firzt just to call 'shop'! at back door when a cuztomer come in, and when growing older to make herseff many other way' uzeful. And by consequence she was oft-en playmate with the chil'ren of all that coterie there in Royal Street. Excep' my father; he was fo'teen year' to her seven."

"Was she a handsome child?" Chester ventured.

"I think no. But in growing up she bic-came"—the craftsman handed out a pocket flash-light and an old carte-de-visite photograph of a black-haired, black-eyed girl of twenty or possibly twenty-three years. "You shall tell me," he said:

"And you'll trust me, my sincerity?"

"Sir! if I di'n' truzt you, ab-so-lutely, you shoul'n' touch that with a finger."

"Well, then, I say yes, she's handsome, trusting you not to gild my plain words with your imagination. She's handsome, but in a way easily overlooked; a way altogether apart from the charms of color and texture, I judge, or of any play of feeling; not floral, not startling, not exquisite; but statuesque, almost heavily so, and replete with the virtues of character."

"Well," said Beloiseau, putting away the picture, "sixteen year' she rimain' rent' to mesdames that way, and come to look lag that. And all of our parent'—gran'parent'—living that simple life like you see us, their descendant', now, she biccame like one of those familie'—Dubroca—Castanado—or of that coterie entire.

"So after while they want' to buy her, to put her free. But Mme. Lefevre she rif-use' any price. She say, 'If Fortune'—that was her name—'would be satisfi' to marry a nize black man like Ovide, who would buy his friddom—ah, yes! But no! If I make her free without, she'll right off want to be marrie' to a white man. Tha'z the only arrengement she'll make with him; she's too piouz for any other arrengement, while same time me I'm too piouz to let her marry a white man; my faith, that would be a crime! And also she coul'n' never be 'appy that way; she's too good and high-mind' to be marrie' to any white man wha'z willin' to marry a nigger.'

"So, then, it come to be said in all those card-club' that my father he's try to buy Fortune so to marry her. An' by that he had a quarrel with one of those young Lefevre', who said pretty much like his mother, only in another manner, pretty insulting. And, same old story, they fought, like we say, 'under those oak,' Métairie Ridge, with sharpen' foil'. And my father he got a bad wound. And he had to be nurse' long time, and biccause all those shop' got to be keep she nurse' him more than everybody elze.

"Well, human nature she's strong. So, when he get well he say, 'Papa, I can' stay any mo' in rue Royale, neither in that vieux carré, neither in that Louisiana.' And my grandpère and all that coterie they say: 'To go at Connect-icut, or Kanzaz, or Californie, tha'z no ril-ief; you muz' go at France and Spain, wherever 'tis good to study the iron-work, whiles we are hoping there will be a renaissance in that art and that businezz; and same time only the good God know' what he can cause to happen to lead a child of the faith out of trouble and sorrow.'

"So my father he went, and by reason of that he di'n' have to settle that queztion of honor what diztress all the balance of the coterie; whether to be on the side of Louisiana, or the Union. He di'n' run away to ezcape that war; he di'n' know 'twas going to be, and he came back in the mi'l' of it, whiles the city was in the han' of that Union army. Also what cause him to rit-urn was not that war. 'Twas one of those thing' what pro-juce' that saying that the truth 'tis mo' stranger than figtion.

110

"Mr. Chezter, 'twas a wonderful! And what make it the mo' wonderful, my father he wasn' hunting for that, neither hadn' ever dream' of it. He was biccome very much a wanderer. One day he juz' chance' to be in a village in Alsace, and there he saw some chil'ren, playing in the street. And he was very thirzty, from long time walking, and he request' them a drink of water. And a li'l' girl fetch' him a drink. But she was modess and di'n' look in his face till he was biggening to drink. Then she look' up—she had only about seven year', and my father he look' down, and he juz' drop that cup by his feet that it broke—the handle. And when she cry, and he talk' with her and say don' cry, he can make a cem-ent juz' at her own house to mend that to a perfegtion, he was astonizh' at her voice as much as her face. And when he ask her name and she tell him, her firz' name, and say tha'z the name of her grand'-mère, he's am-aze'! But when he see her mother meeting them he's not surprise', he's juz' lightning-struck.

"Same time he try to hide that, and whiles he's mixing that cem-ent and sticking that handle he look' two-three time' into the front of the hair of that li'l' girl, till the mother she get agitate', and she h-ask him: 'What you're looking? Who told you to look for something there? Ma foi! you're looking for the pompon gris of my mother and grandmother! You'll not fine it there. Tha'z biccause she's so young; when she's grow' up you'll see; but'—she part' as-ide her own hair in front and he see', my father, under the black a li'l' patch of gray, and he juz' say, 'Mon dieu!' while she egsclaim'—

"'If you know anybody's got that pompon in Louisiana, age of me, or elze, if older, the sizter of my mother, she's lost yonder sinze mo' than twen'y-five year'. My anceztor' they are name' Pompon for that li'l' gray spot.'

"Well, then they—and her 'usband, coming in—they make great frien'. My father he show' them thiz picture, and when he tell them the origin-al of that also is name' Fortune, like that child an' her mother, and been from in-fancy a slave, they had to cry, all of them together. And then they tell my father all ab-out those two sizter', how they get marrie' in that village with two young men, cousin' to each other, and how one pair, a year avter, emigrate' to Louisiana with li'l' baby name' Fortune, and—once mo' that old story—they are bound to the captain of the ship for the prise of the passage till somebody in Ammerica rid-eem them and they are bound to him to work that out. And coming accrozz, the father—ship-fever—die', and arriving, the passage is pay by the devil know' who'.

"Then my father he tell them that chile muz' be orpheline at

111

two-three year', biccause while seeming so white she never think she wasn' black.

"And so my father, coming ad that village the moz' unhappy in the worl', he went away negs day the moz' happy. And he took with him some photo' showing that mother and chile with the mother's hair comb' to egspose that pompon gris; and also he took copy from those record' of babtism of the babtism of that li'l' Fortune, émigré.

"Same time, here at home, our Fortune she was so sick with something the doctor he coul'n' make out the nature, and she coul'n' eat till they're af-raid she'll die. And one day the doctor bring her father confessor, there where she's in bed, and break that gently that my father he's come home, and then that he's bring with him the perfec' proof that she's as white as she look'. Well, negs day she's out of bed; secon' she's dress—and laughing!—and eating! And every day my father he's paying his intention', and Mme. Lefevre she's rij-oice, biccause that riproach is pass' from monsieur her 'usband and pritty quick they are marrie', and tha'z my mother."

After a reverent silence Chester spoke: "And lived long and happily together?"

"Yes, a long, beautiful life. Maybe that life woul'n' be of a diztinction sufficient to you, but to them, yes. They are gone but since lately."

"And that Lefevre house?"

"Ah, you know! Full of Italian'—ten-twelve familie', with washing on street veranda eight day ev'ry week. Pauvre vieux carré!"

XLII

MÉLANIE

"I suppose," Chester said, breaking another silence, "you and that mother, and your father, have sat in the flowery sunshine of this old plaza together——"

"A thousan' time'," the ironworker replied, mused a bit, and added: "My frien', you are a so patient listener as I never see. Biccause I know you are all that time waiting for a differen' story. And now—I shall tell you that?"

112

"Yes, however it hits me I've got to know it."

"Well, after that, a year and half, I am born. I grow up. I 'ave brother' and sizter'. We all get marrie', and they, they are scatter' over the face of Louisiana. But me, I'm the oldest and my father take great trouble in educating me to sugceed him in his businezz, and so I did, like you see. And the same with Dubroca and with Castanado—Ducatel he's different he's come into that antique businezz by his mizfortune and he's—oh, he's all right only he's not of the same inspiration to be of that li'l' clique. He's up-town Creole and with the up-town Creole mind. And those De l'Isle' they also got a son, and Mme. Alexandre she have a very amiable daughter; and, laz', not leazt, you know, those Chapdelaine'——"

"I certainly do," Chester murmured.

"Yes, assuredlie," said Beloiseau. "Well, now: In those generation' befo' there was in Royal Street—and Bourbon—and Dauphine—bisside' crozz-street'—so many of our—I ignore the Englizh word for that—our affinité, that our whole market of mat-rim-ony was not juz' in one square of Royal; but presently, it break out like an épidémique, ammongs' our chil'ren, to marry juz' accrozz and accrozz the street; a Beloiseau to a Castanado, a Castanado to a Dubroca, and so forth—even fifth!" The speaker smiled benignly. "Hah! many year' they work' my geniuz hard to make iron candlestick'—orig-in-al diz-ign—for wedding-present'. The moze of them, they marrie' without any romanze, egcep' what cann' be av-oid', inside the heart, when both partie' are young, and in love together, and not rich neither deztitute. But year biffo' laz' we have the romanze of that daughter of Mme. Alexandre and son of De l'Isle and son of Dubroca."

"Is that Mélanie, whom you all mention so often but whom I've never seen?"

"Yes. Reason you don't see her—— But I'll tell you that. Mr. Chezter, that would make a beautyful story to go with those other' in that book of Mlle. Aline—but of co'se by changing those name', and by preten'ing that happen' at Hong Kong, or Chicago, or Bogota. Presently 'tis too short, but you can easy mazk and coztume that in a splendid rhétorique till it's plenty long enough."

"H'mm!" said Chester, wondering at the artisan's artlessness off his beaten track. "Go on."

"Well, she's not beautyful, Mélanie; same time she's not bad-looking and she's kindess of the kind, and whoever she love'—her mother, for example—and Mlle. Aline—tha'z pretty touching, to see with what an inten-city she love'.

"Now, what I tell you, tha'z a very sicret bitwin you and me.

Biccause even those Dubroca', père and mère, and those De l'Isle', père and mère, they do' know all that; and me I know that only from Castanado, who know' it only from his wife; biccause she, she know' it only from Mlle. Aline, and none of them know that I know egcep' those Castanado'.

"Well! sinze chilehood those three—Mélanie, De l'Isle, Dubroca,—they are playmate' together, and Dubroca he's always call' Mélanie his swit-heart. But De l'Isle, no. Always biffo', those De l'Isle they are of the, eh, the beau monde and though li'l' by li'l' losing their fortune, keeping their frien', some of them rich, yet still ad the same time nize people. And that young De l'Isle he's a good-looking, well-behave', ambitiouz, and got—what you call—dash!

"That was the condition when they are all graduate' from school and go each into his o'cupation, or hers, up to the eyebrow'. Mélanie and Mlle. Aline they work' with Mme. Alexandre, though not precizely together, biccause Mélanie she show' only an ability to keep those account' and to assist keeping shop, whiles Mlle. Aline she rimain' always up-stair' employing that great talent tha'z too valu'ble to be interrupt'."

"Doesn't she keep the books now?"

"Yes, but tha'z only to assist Mélanie whiles Mélanie she's, eh, away. Dubroca he go' into businezz with his father, likewise Castanado with his father, but De l'Isle he's made a secretary in City-hall. So he have mo' time than those other' and he go' oft-en into society, and he get those manner' and cuztom' of society. And then that young Dubroca biggen very plain to pay his intention' to Mélanie, and we are all pretty glad to notiz that, biccause whiles he don't got that dash of De l'Isle, he's modess, yet still brave to a perfegtion; and he's square and got plenty sense, and he's steady and he's kind. Every way they are suit' to each other and we think— if that poor old rue Royale con-tinue to run down, that will even be good to join those two businezz' together. And bisside', sinze a li'l' shaver Dubroca he ain't never love nobody else, only Mélanie.

"But also De l'Isle, like Dubroca, he was always pretty glad of every egscuse to drop in there at Mme. Alexandre and pass word with Mélanie. 'Twas easy to see 'tis to Mlle. Aline he's in love and he come talk to Mélanie biccause tha'z the nearess he can reach to Mlle. Aline egcep' juz' saying good-day whiles passing on street or at church door. Oh, he behave the perfec' gen'leman, and still tha'z one reason she get that li'l' 'Ector. Yes, we all see that, only Mélanie she don't. So Mlle. Aline she ezcape' him all she could, but, with that dash he's got, he persevere' to hang on. And tha'z the miztake they both did, him and Mélanie, in doing that American way, keeping that to themselve' instead of—French way—telling their parent'.

114

"Then another thing tranzpire'. My son and that son of Castanado bigin, both—but that come' mo' later. Any'ow one day Mélanie she bring Mlle. Aline a note from De l'Isle sol-iciting if she and Mélanie will go at matinée with him and Dubroca. And when mademoiselle bigin to make egscuse' Mélanie implore' her to go, biccause Mme. Alexandre say no Creole girl cann' go juz' with one man, or even with two. 'And mamma she's right,' Mélanie say—with tear',—'even in that Am'erican way they got a limit, and same time I'm perishing to go!'

"And when mademoiselle hear' what that play is ab-out she consent' at the lazt to go. Biccause tha'z ab-out a girl what billieve' a man's in love to her, biccause he pay her those li'l' galanterie of high life—li'l' pol-ite figtion'—what every man—-unless he's marrie'—egspect to pay to every girl, to make thing' pleasant, you know?

"And that play turn out a so egcellent that many people, paying admission ad the door, find they got to pay ag-ain, secon' time, ad their seat, in tear' that they weep; and that make it not so hard for Mélanie, who weep ab-out ten price'. Negs day, Sunday, avter church and dinner, she come yonder ad the home of mademoiselle, you know, Bourbon Street, and sit with her in the gol'fish bower of that li'l' garden behine. And she's very much bow' down. And she h-ask mademoiselle if she ain't notiz sinz long time how De l'Isle is paying intention to her, Mélanie. But mademoiselle di'n' have to be embarrazz' what to answer, biccause Mélanie she's so rattle' she don't wait to hear. And Mélanie she say tha'z one cause that she was wanting De l'Isle to see that play; biccause sinz lately she's notiz he's make himseff very complimentary also to mademoiselle, and she, Mélanie, she want' him to notiz how that way he's in danger to make mizunderstanding and diztress to himseff and—all concern'.

"And she prod-uce' a piece paper fill' with memorandum' of compliment' he's say to her one time and other, what she's wrote down whiles frezh spoken and what she billieve' are proof that he's in love to her and inten' to make his proposition so soon he's got good sign' he'll be accept'. 'But I ain't never give' him sign,' she say, 'biccause a girl she cann' never be too careful. And so I think I'm bound to show that to you, biccause I muz'n' be careful only for myseff, and if he's say such thing' likewise to you, then tha'z to be false to both of us together. But, I think,' she say, 'M. De l'Isle he coul'n' never do that!'"

"How did she say all that, angrily or meekly?"

"Oh! meek and weeping till mademoiselle she's compel' to weep likewise. And ad the end she's compel' to tell Mélanie yes, De

115

l'Isle he's pay her those same kind of sentimental plaisanteries; rosebud' to pin on the heart outside, a few minute', till the negs cavalier. Castanado, she say, Beloiseau, they do the same—even more. 'Ah!' Mélanie say, 'but only to you! and only biccause to say any mo' they are yet af-raid! Mademoiselle, those both, they are both in love to you!'

"And when Mélanie say that, Mlle. Aline take the both hand' of Mélanie in her both han' and ask her if she ain't herseff put them both, Castanado, Beloiseau, up to that—to fall in love to her. And pretty soon Mélanie she's compel' to confezz that, not with word', but juz' with the fore-head on the knee of mademoiselle and crying like babie. And she say she's sin'. And yet same time while she h-ask' mademoiselle to pray the good God and the mother of God to forgive that sin, she h-ask her to pray also that they'll make De l'Isle to love her.

"Biccause, she say, 'tis those unfortunate rosebud' of sentimental plaisanterie he give her what firz' make her to love him. And mademoiselle she ag-ree' to that if Mélanie she'll tell that whole story also to her mother; biccause mademoiselle she see what a hole that put them both in, her and Mélanie, when she, mademoiselle, is bound to know he's paying, De l'Isle, all his real intention' to herseff. And Mélanie she's in agonie and say no-no-no! but if mademoiselle will tell it, yes! And by reason that she's kep' that from her mother sinze the firz', she say tell not Mme. Alexandre but Mme. Castanado, even when mademoiselle say if Mme. Castanado then also monsieur; biccause madame she'll certainly make that condition, and biccause monsieur he can assist her to commenze that whole businezz over, French way. And same time Mélanie she take very li'l' stock in that French way, by reason that, avter all, those De l'Isle, though their money's gone, are still pretty high-life.

"And tha'z how it come that those Castanado' have to tell me. Biccause madame she cann' skip ar-ound pretty light, you know, and biccause they think my, eh—pull—with those De l'Isle' is the moze of anybody, and biccause I require to know how they are sure 'tis uzeless any mo' for my son, or their son, than for the son of De l'Isle, to sed the heart on Mlle. Aline. Also tha'z to egsplain me why Mlle. Aline say if all those intention' to her don't finizh righd there, she got to stop coming ad Mme. Alexandre. And of co'se! You see that, I su'pose?"

"And where was young Dubroca in all this?"

"Ah, another migsture! He was nowhere. Any'ow, tha'z how he feel; and those other three boy' they di'n' feel otherwise. You see? We coul'n' egsplain them anything—ab-out Mlle. Aline,—all we can say: 'Road close'—stim-roller.' So ad the end Dubroca he have, slimly, the advantage; for him, to Mélanie, the road any 'ow seem' open; yet in vain. So there, all at same time, in that li'l' gang, rue Royale, was five heart' blidding for love, and nine other' blidding for those five and for Mlle. Aline.

"Well, of co'se—you see?—nobody cann' stand that! Firzt to find his way out of that is Mélanie. Mélanie's confessor he think tha'z a sin to keep any longer those fact' from her mother, and she confezz them to Mme. Alexandre, and ad the end she say: 'Mamma, in our li'l' coterie I cann' look anybody in the face any mo', and I'm going to biccome train' nurse. Tha'z not running away, yet same time tha'z not every evening to be getting me singe' in the same candle.'

"Then, almoze while she saying that, that son of De l'Isle he say to my son—who he's fon' of like a brother, and my son of him likewise, though the one is a so dashing and the other a so quiet—"Oiseau,' he say,—biccause tha'z the nickname of my son,—'papa and me we visit' the French consul to-day and arrange' a li'l' affair.'

"And when he want' to tell some mo' my son he stop' him: 'Enough! I div-ine that. Why you di'n' take me al-ong? You'll arrange to go at that France, of my grand'mère, and that Alsace, of her mother, to be fighting aviateur, and leave 'Oiseau behine? Ah, you cann' do that!' And when that young Dubroca and Castanado get the win' of them, the all four, all of same sweet maladie, they go together; two to be juz' poilu', two, aviateur'. That old remedie, you know; if they can't love—they'll fight! They are yonder, still al-ive, laz' account."

Mainly to himself Chester said, "And I am here, my land still at peace, last account."

"And also you, you've h-ask' mademoiselle, I think," said the ironworker, "and alas, she's say aggain, no, eh?"

The reply was a gaze and a nod.

"Well, Mr. Chezter, I'm sorrie! Her reason—you can't tell. 'Tis maybe juz' biccause those hero' are yonder. 'Tis maybe only that those two aunt' are here. Maybe 'tis biccause both, maybe neither. You can't tell. Maybe you h-ask too soon. Ad the present she know' you only sinze a few week'. She don't know none of yo' hiztorie, neither yo' familie—egcep' that h-angel of the Lord. Yo' char-acter, she may like that very well yet same time she know' how easy that is for women to make miztake' about. Maybe y'ought to 'ave ask' M'sieu' Thorndyke-Smith to write at yo' home-town and get you recommen'. Even a cook he's got to 'ave that—or a publisher, eh?"

"I've got that—within reach; my law firm has it. But, pshaw! I

117

think, Beloiseau, while all your maybe's may be right the thing that explains mademoiselle's whole situation is that she's never seen a man worthy to touch a hem of her robe; and the only argument a lover can lay at her feet is that she never will."

"And you'll lay that, negs time?"

"Not till that manuscript business is settled, don't you see? Come, you must go to bed."

XLIII

Shrimps, rice, and watered wine for a sunset dinner. At its end the three Chapdelaines, each with her small cup of black coffee, left the table and its remnants to the other two members of the household, and passed out as usual to the bower benches and the goldfish pool.

Humming-birds were there, drinking frenziedly from honeysuckle cups to the health of all things beautiful and ecstatic. Mlle. Yvonne stood at a bench's end to watch one of them dart from bloom to bloom. "Ah, Corinne," she sighed, "if we could all be juz' humming-bird'!"

"Chérie," cried her sister, "you are spilling yo' coffee!"

Whether for the coffee, for the fact that we can't all be humming-birds, or for some thought not yet spoken, Mlle. Corinne's eyes were all but spilling their tears. As the trio sat down. Aline said in gentlest accusation to the younger aunt:

"You are trembling. Why is that?"

The younger sister looked appealingly to the elder. "Chère," Mlle. Corinne said to the girl, "we are anxiouz to confezz you something. We woul'n' never be anxiouz to confezz that, only we're af-raid already you've foun' us out!"

"Yes. I came this evening by Ovide's shop to return a book—"

"An' he tell you he's meet us——?"

"On the steps of the archevêché."

"Ah, chèrie," Yvonne tearfully broke in, "can you ever pardon that to us?"

Aline smiled: "Oh, yes; in the course of time, I suppose. That was not like a drinking-saloon."

"Ah-h! not in the leas'! We di'n' touch there a drop—nobodie di'n' offer us!"

The niece addressed the other aunt: "Go on. Tell me why you were there."

"Aline, we'll confess us! We wend there biccause—we are orphan'! Of co'se, we know that biffo', sinze long time, many, many year'; but only sinze a few day'——"

"Joy-ride day," Aline put in, a bit tensely.

"Ah, no! Chérie, you muz' not supose——"

"Never mind; 'last few days'—go on."

"Well, sinze those laz' few day' we bigin to feel like we juz' got to take step' ab-oud that!"

"So you took those steps of the archevêché."

"Chère, we'll tell you! Yvonne and me, avter all those many 'appy year' with you, we think we want—ah, chérie, you'll pardon that?—we want ad the laz' to live independent! So we go ad the archbishop. And he say, 'How I'm going to make you that? You think to be independent by biccoming Sizter' of Charitie—of Mercy—of St. Joseph?'

"'Ah, no,' we say, 'we have not the geniuz to be those; not even to be Li'l'-Sizter'-of-the-Poor. All we want—and we coul'n' make ourselv' the courage to ask you that, only we've save' you so large egspenses not asking you that already sinze twenty-thirty year' aggo—we want you to put us in orphan asylum.' We was af-raid at firz' he's goin' to be mad; but he smile very kine and say: 'Yes, yes; you want, like the good Lord say, to biccome like li'l' children, eh?'

"'Ah, yes!' we tell him, 'tha'z what we be glad to do. They got nothing in the worl' we can do, Yvonne and me, so easy like that! And same time we be no egspense, like those li'l' orpheline'; we can wash dish', make bed', men' apron'; and in that way we be independent!' Well, he scratch his head; yet same time he smile', while he say, 'Go, li'l' children, to yo' home. I'll see if Mère Veronique can figs that, and if yes, I'll san' for you.' And, chérie, juz' the way he said that, we are sure he's goin' to san'."

With her tears running freely Aline softly laughed. She rose, took a hand of each aunt, laid the two together, bent low, and kissed them, saying: "He will not, for he shall not. Nothing shall ever part us but heaven."

XLIV

One evening M. Castanado sat reading to his wife from a fresh number of the weekly Courier des Etats-Unis.

It was not long after the incident last mentioned. Chester had become accustomed to his new lift in fortune, but as yet no further word as to the manuscript had reached him; he had only just written a second letter of inquiry after it. Also that summons to the two aunts, from the archbishop, of which the pair were so sure, was still unheard; no need had arisen for Aline to take any counter-step. We could name the exact date, for it was the day of the week on which the Courier always came, and the week was the last in which a Canal Street movie-show beautifully presented the matchless Bernhardt as a widowed shopkeeper—like Mme. Alexandre, but with a son, not daughter, in love.

The door-bell rang. Castanado went down to the street. There, letting in a visitor, he spoke with such animation that madame, listening from her special seat, guessed, and before the two were half up-stairs knew, who it was. It was Mélanie Alexandre.

No one answered her mother's bell, she said, kissing madame lingeringly, twice on the forehead and once on either vast cheek. She was short and square, with such serene kindness of face and voice as to be the last you would ever pick out to fall into a mistake of passion, however exalted. Of course, that serenity may have come since the mistake. Both Castanados seemed to take note of it as if it had come since, and she to be willing they should note it.

"No," they said, "Mme. Alexandre had gone with Dubroca and his wife to that movie of Sarah."

"And also with M. Beloiseau?" asked Mélanie, with a lurking smile, as she sat down so fondly close to madame as to leave both her small hands in one of her friend's.

"Ah, now," madame exclaimed, "there is nothing in that! You ought to be rijoice' if there was."

The new look warmed in Mélanie's eyes. "I'll be very glad if that time ever comes," she said.

"Then you billieve in the second love?"

"Ah, in a case like that! Indeed, yes. In their first love they both were happy; the second would be in praise of the first."

"And to separate them there is only the street," Castanado suggested, "and Royal Street, street of their birth and chilehood, and so narrow, it have the effect to join, not separate. But!"—he made a wary motion—"kip quite, eize they will not go into the net, those old bird', hah!"

There was a smiling silence, and then—"Well," madame said, "they are all to stop here as they riturn. Waiting here, you'll see them all."

"Yes, and beside', I have some good news for you; news anyhow to me."

The pair smiled brightly: "You 'ave another letter from Dubroca!"

"Yes. He's again wounded and in hospital."

"Oh-h, terrible! tha'z to you good news?"

"Yes. Look, monsieur; he has, at the front, the chance to be hit so many times. If he's hit and only wounded his chances to be hit again are made one less, eh? And while he's in hospital they are again two or three less. Shall we not be glad for that? And moreover, how he got his wound, that is better. He got that taking, by himself, nine Boches! And still the best news is what he writes about his friend Castanado."

"Ah, Mélanie! And you hold that back till now? And you know we are without news of him sinze a month! He's promote'? He's decorate'?"

"He's found a treasure. I think maybe you'll get his letter to-morrow. Me, I got mine soon; passing the post-office I went in and asked."

"But how, he found a treasure? and what sort?"

"He just happened to dig it up, in a cellar, in Rheims. He's betrothed.'

"Mélanie! What are you saying?"

"What he says. And that's all he says. I hope you'll hear all about that to-morrow."

"Oh, any'ow tha'z the bes' of news!" Castanado said, kissing his wife's hand and each temple. "Doubtlezz he's find some lovely orphan of that hideouz war; we can trus' his good sense, our son. But, Mélanie, he muz' have been sick, away from the front, to make that courtship."

"I do not know. Everything happens terribly fast these days. I hope you'll hear all about that to-morrow."

Castanado playfully lifted a finger: "Mélanie, how is that, you pass that poss-office, when it is up-town, while you—?" The question hung unfinished—maybe because Mélanie turned so red, maybe because the door-bell rang again.

Enlivened by the high art they had been enjoying and by the fresh night air, a full half-dozen came in: M. and Mme. De l'Isle,

121

whom the others had chanced upon as they left the theatre; Dubroca and his wife; Mme. Alexandre; and finally Beloiseau. "Mélanie!" was the cry of each of these as he or she turned from saluting madame; this was one of madame's largest joys; to get early report from larger or smaller fractions of the coterie, on the good things they had seen or heard, from which her muchness otherwise debarred her. The De l'Isles, however, were not such a matter of course as the others, and Mme. De l'Isle, as she greeted Mme. Castanado, said, in an atmosphere that trembled with its load of mingled French and English:

"We got something to show you!"

In the same atmosphere—"And how got you away from yo' patient?" Mme. Alexandre asked her daughter as they embraced a second time.

"I tore myself," said Mélanie, while Castanado, to all the rest, was saying:

"And such great news as Mél'——"

But a sharp glance from Mélanie checked him. "Such great news as we have receive'! Our son is bethroath'!—to a good, dizcreet, beautiful French girl; which he foun', in a cellar at Rheims!" When a drum-fire of questions fell on him he grew reticent and answered quietly: "We have only that by firz' letter. Full particular' pretty soon, perchanze to-morrow."

"Then to-morrow we'll come hear ab-out it," Beloiseau said, "and tell ab-out the movie. Mme. De l'Isle she's also got fine news, what she cann' tell biffo' biccause"—he waved to Mme. De l'Isle to say why, but her husband spoke for her.

"Biccause," he said, "'tis all in a pigture, war pigture, on a New York Sunday paper, and of co'se we coul'n' stop under street lamp for that; and with yo' permission"—to Mme. Castanado—"we'll show that firz' of all to Scipion."

Beloiseau put on glasses and looked. "'General Joffre—'" he began to read.

"No, no! not that! This one, where you know the général only by the back of his head."

"Ah—ah, yes; 'Two aviateur' riceiving from General Joffre'—my God! De l'Isle—my God! madame,"—Scipion pounded his breast with the paper—"they are yo' son and mine!"

The company rushed to his elbows. "My faith! Castanado, there are their name'! and 'For destrugtion of their eighteenth enemy aeroplane, under circumstance' calling for exceptional coolnezz and intrepid-ity!'"

There was great and general rejoicing and some quite

122

pardonable boasting, under cover of which Mélanie and her mother slipped out by the inside way, without mention of the young Dubroca, his prisoners, sickness, or letter, except to his father and mother, who told of him more openly when the Alexandres were safely gone. That brought fresh gladness and praise, a fair share of which was for Mélanie.

So presently the remaining company vanished, leaving Mme. Castanado free to embrace her kneeling husband and boast again the power of prayer.

XLV

The cathedral that year was undergoing repairs.

Its cypress-log foundations, which had kept sound from colonial days in a soil always wet, had begun to decay when a new drainage system began to dry it out. Fact, but also allegory.

It may have been in connection with this work, or with some change in the house of the Discalceated Sisters of Mt. Carmel, or of the archbishop, or of St. Augustine's Church, that a certain priest of exceptional taste, Beloiseau's father confessor, dropped in on him to order an ornamental wrought-iron grille for the upper half of a new door. While looking at patterns he asked:

"And what is the latest word from your son?"

Scipion showed him that picture—he had bought one for himself—the dear old unmistakable back of "Papa Joffre," and the dear young unmistakable faces of the two boys, Beloiseau and De l'Isle.

A talk followed, on the conflict between a father's pride and his yearning to see his only son safely delivered from constant deadly peril. They spoke of Aline. Not for the first time; Scipion, unaware that the good father was her confessor also, had told him before of his son's hopeless love, to ask if it was not right for him, the father, to help Chester win the marvellous girl, since winning would win the two boys home again.

Patterns waited while the ironworker said that to the tender chagrin of all the coterie Chester was refused—a man of such fineness, such promise, mind, charm, and integrity, and so fitted for her in years, temperament, and tastes, that no girl, however perfect, could hope to be courted by more than one such in a lifetime.

In brief Creole prose he struck the highest key of Shakespeare's sonnets: "Was she not doing a grievous wrong to herself and Chester, to the whole coterie that so adored her, especially to the De l'Isles and himself, and even to society at large? Her reasons," he said, shifting to English, "I can guess at them, but guessing at 'alf-a-dozen convinze' me of none!"

"Have you guess' at differenze of rilligious faith?" the priest inquired.

"Yes, but—nothing doing; I 'ave to guess no."

"Tha'z a great matter to a good Catholic."

"Ah, father! Or-din-arily, yes. Bud this time no. Any'ow, this time tha'z not for us Catholic' to be diztress' ab-out. . . . Ah, yes, chil'ren. But, you know? If daughter', they'll be of the faith and conduc' of the mother; if son', faith of the mother, conduc' of the father; and I think with that even you, pries' of God, be satizfie', eh?

"My dear frien', you know what I billieve? Me, I billieve in heaven they are waiting impatiently for that marriage."

The priest may have been professionally delinquent, but he chose to leave the argument unrefuted. He smilingly looked at his watch. "Well," he said, "I choose this design. Make it so. Good evening." He turned away. Beloiseau called after him, but the man of God kept straight on.

The ironworker loitered back to where the chosen pattern lay, and stood over it still thinking of Chester. Presently a soft voice sounded so close by that he turned abruptly. At his side was an extremely winsome stranger. His artistic eye instantly remarked not only her well-preserved beauty, but its gentle dignity, rare refinement, and untypical quality. Whether it was Creole or Américain, Southern, Northern, or Western, nothing betrayed; on the surface at least, the provincial, as far as the ironworker could see, was wholly bred out of her. He noted also the unimpaired excellence of her erect and girlish slightness and, under her pretty hat and early whitened hair, the carven fineness of her features. Her whole attire pleasantly befitted her years, which might have been anything short of fifty; and yet, if Scipion was right, she might have dressed for thirty.

"Are you Mr. Beloiseau?" she inquired.

"I am," he said.

"Mr. Beloiseau, I'm the mother of Geoffry Chester. You know him, I believe?"

"Oh, is that possible? He is my esteem' frien', madame. Will you"—he began to dust a lone chair.

"No, thank you; I came to find Geoffry's quarters. I left the hotel with my memorandum, but must have dropped it. I remember only Bienville Street."

"He's not there any mo'. Sinze only two day' he's move'. Mrs. Chezter, if you'll egscuse me till I can change the coat I'll show you those new quarter'. Whiles I'm changing you can look ad that book of pattern', and also—here—there's a pigtorial of New York; that—tha'z of my son and the son of my neighbor up-stair', De l'Isle, ric'iving medal' from Général Joffre——"

"Why, Mr. Beloiseau can it be!"

"But you know, Mrs. Chezter, he's not there presently, yo' son. He's gone at St. Martinville, to the court there."

"Yes, to be back to-morrow or next day. They told me in his office this forenoon. I reached the city only at eleven, train late. He didn't know I was coming. My telegram's on his desk unopened. But having time, I thought I'd see whether he's living comfortably or only fancies he is."

On their way Mrs. Chester and her guide hardly spoke until Scipion asked: "Madame, when you was noticing yo' telegram on the desk of yo' son you di'n' maybe notiz' a letter from New York? We are prettie anxiouz for that to come to yo' son. I do' know if you know about that or no, but M. De l'Isle and madame, and Castanado and his madame, and Dubroca and his madame, and Mme. Alexandre and me, and three Chapdelaine', we are all prettie anxiouz for that letter."

"Yes, I know about it, and there is one, from a New York publishing-house, on Geoffry's desk."

"Well, madame, Marais Street, here's the place. Ah! and street-car—or jitney—passing thiz corner will take you ag-ain at yo' hotel."

XLVI

Satisfied with her son's quarters, Mrs. Chester returned to her hotel and had just dined when her telephone rang.

"Mme.—oh, Mme. De l'Isle, I'm so please'——"

The instrument reciprocated the pleasure. "If Mrs. Chezter was not too fat-igue' by travelling, monsieur and madame would like to call."

Soon they appeared and in a moment whose brevity did honor to both sides had established cordial terms. Rising to go, the pair asked a great favor. It made them, they said, "very 'appy to perceive that Mr. Chezter, by writing, has make his mother well acquaint' with that li'l' coterie in Royal Street, in which they, sometime', 'ave the honor to be include'." "The honor" meant the modest condescension, and when Mrs. Chester's charming smile recognized the fact the pair took fresh delight in her. "An' that li'l' coterie, sinze hearing that from Beloiseau juz' this evening, are anxiouz to see you at ones; they are, like ourselve', so fon' of yo' son; and they cannot call all together—my faith, that would be a procession! And bi-side', Mme. Castanado she—well—you understan' why that is—she never go' h-out. Same time M. Castanado he's down-stair' waiting——

"Shall I go around there with you? I'll be glad to go." They went.

Through that "recommend'" of Chester, got by Thorndyke-Smith for the law firm, and by him shown to M. De l'Isle, the coterie knew that the pretty lady whom they welcomed in Castanado's little parlor was of a family line from which had come three State governors, one of whom had been also his State's chief justice. One of her pleasantest impressions as she made herself at ease among them, and they around her and Mme. Castanado, was that they regarded this fact as honoring all while flattering none. She found herself as much, and as kindly, on trial before them as they before her, and saw that behind all their lively conversation on such comparatively light topics as the World War, greater New Orleans, and the decay of the times, the main question was not who, but what, she was. As for them, they proved at least equal to the best her son had ever written of them.

And they found her a confirmation of the best they had ever discerned in her son. In her fair face they saw both his masculine beauty and the excellence of his mind better interpreted than they had seen them in his own countenance. A point most pleasing to them was the palpable fact that she was in her son's confidence. Evidently, though arriving sooner than expected, her coming was due to his initiative. Clearly he had written things that showed a juncture wherein she, if but prompt enough, might render the last great service of her life to his. Oh, how superior to the ordinary American slap-dash of the matrimonial lottery! They felt that they themselves had taken the American way too much for granted. Maybe that was where they were unlike Mlle. Aline. But she was not there, to perceive these things, nor her aunts, to be seen and estimated. The evening's outcome could be but inconclusive, but it was a happy beginning.

Its most significant part was a brief talk following the mention of the Castanado soldier-boy's engagement. His expected letter had come, bringing many pleasant particulars of it, and the two parents were enjoying a genuine and infectious complacency. "And one thing of the largez' importanze, Mrs. Chezter," madame said with sweet enthusiasm, "—the two they are of the one ril-ligion!"

Was the announcement unlucky, or astute? At any rate it threw the subject wide open by a side door, and Mrs. Chester calmly walked in.

"That's certainly fortunate," she said. Every ear was alert and Beloiseau was suddenly eager to speak, but she smilingly went on: "It's true that, coming of a family of politicians, and being pet daughter—only one—of a judge, I may be a trifle broad on that point. Still I think you're right and to be congratulated."

The whole coterie felt a glad thrill. "Ah, madame," Beloiseau exclaimed, "you are co'rec'! But, any'ow, in a caze where the two faith' are con-tra-ry 'tis not for you Protestant' to be diztres' ab-out! You, you don' care so much ab-out those myzterie' of bil-ief as about those rule' of conduc'. Almoze, I may say, you run those rule' of conduc' into the groun'—and tha'z right! And bis-ide', you 'ave in everything—politic', law, trade, society—so much the upper han'—in the bes' senze—ah, of co'se in the bes' senze!—that the chil'ren of such a case they are pretty sure goin' to be Protestant!"

Mrs. Chester, having her choice, to say either that marriages across differences of faith had peculiar risks, or that Geoffry's uncle, the "Angel of the Lord," had married, happily, a Catholic, chose neither, let the subject be changed, and was able to assure the company that the missive on Geoffry's desk was no bulky manuscript, but a neat thin letter under one two-cent stamp.

"Accept'!" they cried, "that beautiful true story of 'The 'Oly Crozz' is accept'! Mesdemoiselles they have strug the oil!"

Mme. Castanado had a further conviction:

"'Tis the name of it done that! They coul'n' rif-use that name!—and even notwithstanding that those publisher' they are maybe Protestant!"

The good nights were very happy. The last were said five squares away, at the hotel, to which the De l'Isles brought her back afoot. "And to-morrow evening, four o'clock," madame said, "I'll come and we'll go make li'l' visite at those Chapdelaine'."

Mrs. Chester had but just removed her hat when again the telephone; from the hotel office—"Your son is here. Yes, shall we send him up?"

XLVII

With hands under their gray sleeves two white-bonneted religieuses turned into Bourbon Street and rang the Chapdelaines' street bell.

Mlle. Yvonne flutteringly let them into the garden, Mlle. Corinne into the house. The conversation was in English, for, though Sister Constance was French, Sister St. Anne, young, fair, and the chief speaker, was Irish. They came from Sister Superior Veronique, they said, to see further about mesdemoiselles entering, eh——

Smilingly mesdemoiselles fluttered more than ever. "Ah, yes, yes! Well, you know, sinze we talk ab-out that with the archbishop we've talk' ab-out it with our niece al-so, and we think she's got to get marrie' befo' we can do that, biccause to live al-lone that way she's too young. But we 'ave the 'ope she's goin' to marry, and then!"

"Have you made a will?"

"Will! Ah, we di'n' never think of that! Tha'z a marvellouz we di'n' never think of that—when we are the two-third' owner' of that lovely proprity there! And we think tha'z always improving in cozt, that place, biccause so antique an' so pittoresque. And if Aline she marrie' and we, we join that asylum doubtlezz Aline she'll be rij-oice' to combine with us to leave that lovely proprity ad the lazt to the church! Biccause, you know, to take that to heaven with us, tha'z impossible, and the church tha'z the nearez' we can come." Odd as the moment seemed for them, tears rolled down their smiling faces.

"But"—they dried their eyes—"there's another thing also bisside'. We are, all three, the authorezz' of a story that we are prettie sure tha'z accept' by the publisher'; an' of co'ze if tha'z accept'—and if those publisher' they don' swin'le us, like so offten—we don't need to be orphan' never any mo', and we'll maybe move up-town and juz' keep that proprity here for a souvenir of our in-fancy. But that be two-three days yet biffo' we can be sure ab-oud that. Maybe ad the laz' we'll 'ave to join the asylum, but tha'z our hope, to move up town into the quartier nouveau and that beautiful 'garden diztric'.' But we'll always con-tinue to love the old 'ouse here. 'Tis a very genuine ancient relique, that 'ouse. You see those wall'? Solid plank of two inch' and from Kentucky!" They went through the whole story—the house, the relics of their childhood— "Go you, Yvonne, fedge them!"

The meek religieuses did their best to be both interested and sincere, but somehow found diplomacy to escape the "li'l' lake" and its goldfish, and even took the piety of the cat with a dampening absence of mind. Their departure was almost hurried. There was nothing to do on either side, the four agreed, but to wait the turn of events.

The two gray robes and white bonnets had but just got away when the bell rang again and Mlle. Yvonne let in Mme. De l'Isle and Mrs. Chester.

But these calls were in mid-afternoon. The evening previous—"Show Mr. Chester to three-thirty-three," the hotel clerk had said, and presently Mrs. Chester was all but perishing in the arms of her son.

"Geoffry! Geoffry! you needn't be ferocious!"

They took seats facing each other, low seats that touched; but when they joined hands a second time he dropped to his knees, asking many questions already answered in her regular and frequent letters. News is so different by word of mouth when the mouth's the sweetest, sacredest ever kissed. "And how's father?"

As if he didn't know to the last detail!

All at once—"Why didn't you say you were coming?" he savagely demanded.

"No matter," his mother replied, "I'm glad I didn't, things have happened so pleasantly. I've seen your whole Royal Street coterie, except, of course——"

"Yes, of course."

The mother told her evening's experience.

"And you like my friends?"

"Why, Geoffry, you're right to love them. But, now, how came you back so soon from St. What's-his-name?"

"Opposing counsel compromised the case without trial. Mother, it's the greatest professional victory I've ever won."

"Oh, how fine! Geoffry, how are you getting on, professionally, anyhow?"

"Better than my best hope, dear; far better. I've shot right up!"

"Then why do you look so weary and care-worn?"

"I don't. I'm older, that's all, dear."

"Oh! Prospering and care-free, and yet you'd drop everything and go to France, to war."

"No, dearie, no. I'm sorry I wrote you what I did, but I only said I felt like it. I don't now. I envied those Royal Street boys, who could do that with a splendid conscience. I—I can't. I can't go killing men, even murderers, for a remote personal reason. I must wait till my own country calls and my patriotism is pure patriotism. That's higher honor—to her, isn't it?"

129

"It is to you; I'm not bothering about her."

"You will when you see her, first sight. To-morrow afternoon, you say. Wish I could be there when your eyes first light on her! Mother, dearie, isn't it as much she as I you've come to see?"

"Well, if it is, what then?"

"I'm glad. But I draw the line at seeing. Help, you understand, I don't want—I won't have!"

"Why, Geoffry, I——!"

"Oh, I say it because there isn't one of that kind-hearted coterie who hasn't wanted to put in something in my favor. I forbid! A dozen to one—I won't allow it! No, nor any two to one, not even we two. Win or lose, I go it alone. 'Twould be fatal to do otherwise if I would. You'll see that the minute you see her."

"Why, Geoffry! What a heat!"

"Oh, I'll be the only one burned. Good night. I can't see you to-morrow before evening. Shall we dine here?"

"Yes. Oh, Geoffry—that New York letter! Manuscript accepted?"

A shade crossed the son's brow. "Don't you think I ought to tell her first?"

"Her first," the mother—the mother—repeated after him. "Maybe so; I don't care." They kissed. "Good night."

"Good night . . . good night . . . good night, dear, darling mother. Good night!"

XLVIII

At the batten door of her high, tight garden-fence Mlle. Yvonne, we repeat, let in Mme. De l'Isle and Mrs. Chester.

"Mother of—ah-h-h!" Her rapture was mated to such courteous restraint that dinginess and dishevelment were easily overlooked. "And 'ow marvellouz that is, that you 'appen to come juz' when he—and us—we're getting that news of the manu'——"

"What! accepted?"

"Oh, that we di'n' hear yet! We only hear he's hear' something, but we're sure tha'z the only something he can hear!" She had begun to close the gate, but Mrs. Chester lingered in it.

"That fine large house and garden across the way," she said, "are they a Creole type?"

"Yes, bez' kind—for in the city. They got very few like that in the vieux carré, but up yonder in that beautiful garden diztric' of the nouveau quartier are many, where we'll perchanze go to live some day pritty soon. That old 'ouse we're inhabiting here, tha'z—like us, ha, ha!—a pritty antique. Tha'z mo' suit' for a relique than to live in, especially for Tantine—ha, ha!—tha'z auntie, yet tha'z what we call our niece. Aline—juz' in plaisanterie!—biccause she take' so much mo' care of us than us of her."

Mrs. Chester had stopped to look around her. "Whenever you move," she said, "you'll have to leave this delightful little garden behind; it won't fit out of these quaint surroundings."

"Ah! We won't want that any mo'!"

They pressed on. "That 'ouse acrozz street," said Mme. De l'Isle, "I notiz there the usual sign."

"Ah, yes, yes! 'For Sale or Rent'; tha'z what always predominate' in that poor vieux carré. But here is my sizter. Corinne, Mrs. Chezter, the mother of Mr. Chezter—as you see by the image of him in the face! I can have the boldnezz to say that, madame, biccause never in my life I di'n' see a young man so 'andsome like yo' son!"

The mother blushed—a lifelong failing. "At home," she said, "he's called his father's double."

"Is that possible? But tha'z the way with people. Some people they find Aline the image of Corinne, and some of me. Yet Corinne and me—look!"

The four went in—to the usual entertainment: the solid plank walls, the fine absence of lath and plaster, Aline's "li'l' robe of baptism," and the bridegroom and bride who had gone a lifetime without a change of linen. They passed out into the rear garden and told wonderful stories of those gifted little darlings the goldfish. Hector, unfortunately absent, had a mouth-organ, to whose strains the fishes would listen so motionless that you could see they were spellbound. Yvonne ran back into the house to get it, but for some cause returned with nerves so shaken that the fishes would do nothing but run wildly to and fro. Still, that was just as startling proof of their amazing whatever-it-was!

Seats were not taken in the bower. The declining sun filled it. Mrs. Chester moved fondly from one flower-bed to another, and while the sisters eagerly filled her hands with their choicest bloom Yvonne privately got a disturbed glance to Corinne that drew the four indoors again. There the outside quaintness tempted Mrs. Chester at once to a front window, with Mlle. Yvonne at her side.

131

The front garden was not as the visitor had seen it shortly before while entering. She turned silently away, while mademoiselle, as though surprised, cried to her sister and Mme. De l'Isle: "Ah! Aline she's arrive'! Mrs. Chezter, 'ow tha'z fortunate for us all!"

So with the other three Mrs. Chester looked out again. Halfway up the walk stood Aline. Her back was to the house. Cupid was just inside the gate, and between them, closely confronting her, was a third figure—Geoffry Chester. The indoor company could see his face, but not its mood, so dazzling was the low sun behind him; but certainly it was not gay. Her hand lay in his through some parting speech, but fell from it as both returned toward the gate. Which Cupid opened—sad irony—for Chester, and while the child locked him out Aline came forward wrapped in sunlight.

By steps, as she came, her beauty of form, face, and soul grew on Mrs. Chester's sight, and when, in the house, with her sunset halo quenched and her presence more perfectly humanized, her smile and voice crowned the revelation, it happened as Geoffry had said it would; the mother's heart went out to her in fond and complete acceptance.

To the four women taking seats with her the laying of a graceful hat off her dark hair was the dissolving of one lovely picture into another unmarred by the fact that a letter which she held in her fingers was the publishers' latest word to Chester. But now, as her own silent gaze fell on it held in her lap in both hands, so did theirs, till her fingers shook and she bit her lip. Then—"Never mind to read it, chère," Mme. De l'Isle said, "juz' tell us. We are prepare' for the worz'. They want to poz'pone the pewblication, or they don't want to pay in advanz'?"

Aline lifted so bright a smile through her tears that every heart grew lighter. "They don't want it at all," she said. "They have sent it back!"

"Oh-h-h! Impossible!" exclaimed the two sisters, their eyes filling. "The clerk he's put the wrong letter—letter for another party!"

Aline smiled again. "No; Mr. Chester, he has the manuscript. Ah, you poor"—again she smiled, biting her lip and wiping her tears. Then she turned, looked steadfastly into Mrs. Chester's face, and suddenly handed her the missive. "Read it out."

Mrs. Chester did so. As history, it said, the paper's interest was too merely encyclopaedic for magazine use, while as romance it was too much a story of peoples, not persons; romantic yet not romance. As to book form the same drawbacks held, besides the fact

132

that there was not enough of it, not one-fifth enough, for even a small book.

When the reader would have handed the letter back it was agreed instead that she should give it to her son. "What does he purpose to do?" she inquired. "This is the judgment of but one publisher, and there are——"

"In the North," Mme. De l'Isle broke in, "they got mo' than a dozen pewblisher'!"

"Whiles one," the sisters pleaded, "tha'z all we require!"

"I know that," said Aline to the four. "'Twas of that we were speaking at the gate. But"—to Mrs. Chester—"that judgment of the one publisher is become our judgment also. So this evening he will bring you the manuscript, and in two or three days, when we come to see you, my two aunt' and me—I, you can give it me."

"May I read it? I've been to Ovide's and read 'The Clock in the Sky.'"

"Yes? Well, if later we have the good, chance to find, in our vieux carré, we and our cotérie, and Ovide, some more stories, true romances, we'll maybe try again; but till then—ah, no."

Mrs. Chester touched the girl caressingly. "My dear, you will! Every house looks as if it could tell at least one, including that large house and garden just over the way."

"Ah," chanted Mlle. Yvonne, "how many time' Corinne and me, we want' to live there and furnizh, ourseff, that romanz'!"

The five rose. Mrs. Chester "would be delighted to have the three Chapdelaines call. I'm leaving the hotel, you know; I've taken a room next Geoffry's. But that's nearer you, is it not?"

"A li'l', yes," the sisters replied, but Aline's smiling silence said: "No, a little farther off."

The aunts thanked Mme. De l'Isle for bringing Mrs. Chester and kissed her cheeks. They walked beside her to the gate, led by Cupid with the key, and by Marie Madeleine crooking the end of her tail like a floor-walker's finger. Mrs. Chester and Aline came last. The sisters ventured out to the sidewalk to finish an apology for a significant fault in Marie Madeleine's figure, and Mrs. Chester and Aline found themselves alone.

"Au revoir," they said, clasping hands. Cupid, under a sudden inspiration, half-closed the gate, the pair stood an eloquent moment gazing eye to eye, and then——

What happened the mother told her son that evening as they sat alone on a moonlit veranda.

"Mother!"

"Yes," she said, "and on the lips."

XLIX

Beginning at dawn, an all-day rain rested the travel-wearied lady. But the night cleared and in the forenoon that followed she shopped—for things, she wrote her husband, not to be found elsewhere in the forty-eight States.

The afternoon she gave to two or three callers, notably to Mrs. Thorndyke-Smith, who was very pleasing every way, but in nothing more than in her praises of the Royal Street coterie. Next morning, in a hired car, she had Castanado and Mme. Dubroca, Beloiseau and Mme. Alexandre, not merely show but, as the ironworker said, pinching forefinger and thumb together in the air, "elucidate" to her, for hours, the vieux carré. The day's latter half brought Mlles. Corinne and Yvonne; but Aline—no.

"She was coming till the laz' moment," the pair said, "and then she's so bewzy she 'ave to sen' us word, by 'Ector, 'tis impossib' to come—till maybe later. Go h-on, juz' we two."

They sat and talked, and rose and talked, and—sweetly importuned—resumed seats and talked, of infant days and the old New Orleans they loved so well, unembarrassed by a maze of innocent anachronisms, and growingly sure that Aline would come.

When at sunset they took leave Mrs. Chester, to their delight, followed to the sidewalk, drifted on by a corner or two, and even turned up Rampart Street, though without saying that it was by Rampart Street her son daily came—walked—from his office. It had two paved ways for general traffic, with a broad space between, where once, the sisters explained, had been the rampart's moat but now ran the electric cars! "You know what that is, rampart? Tha'z in the 'Star-Spangle' Banner' ab-oud that. And this high wall where we're passing, tha'z the Carmelite convent, and—ah! ad the last! Aline! Aline!" Also there was Cupid.

The four encountered gayly. "Ah, not this time," Aline said. "I came only to meet my aunts; they had locked the gate! But I will call, very soon."

They walked up to the next corner, the sisters confusingly instructing Mrs. Chester how to take a returning street-car. Leaving them, she had just got safely across from sidewalk to car-track when Cupid came pattering after, to bid her hail only the car marked "Esplanade Belt."

As he backed off—"Take care!" was the cry, but he sprang the wrong way and a hurrying jitney cast him yards distant, where he lay unconscious and bleeding. The packed street-car emptied.

"No, he's alive," said one who lifted him, to the two jitney passengers, who pushed into the throng. "Arm broke', yes, but he's hurt worst in the head."

There was an apothecary's shop in sight. They put him and the four ladies into the jitney and sent them there, and the world moved on.

At the shop he came to, and presently, in the jitney again, he was blissfully aware of Geoffry Chester on the swift running-board, questioning his mother and Aline by turns. He listened with all his might. Neither the child nor his mistress had seen or heard the questioner since the afternoon he was locked out of the garden.

Nearing that garden now, questions and answers suddenly ceased; the child had spoken. Limp and motionless, with his head on Aline's bosom and his eyes closed, "Don't let," he brokenly said, "don't let him go 'way."

To him the answer seemed so long coming that he began to repeat; then Aline said——

"No, dear, he shan't leave you."

The sisters had telephoned their own physician from the apothecary's shop, and soon, with Cupid on his cot, pushed close to a cool window looking into the rear garden, and the garden lighted by an unseen moon, Mrs. Chester, at the cot's side awaited the doctor's arrival. The restless sisters brought her a tray of rusks and butter and tea, though they would not, could not, taste anything themselves until they should know how gravely the small sufferer— for now he began to suffer—was hurt.

"Same time tha'z good to be induztriouz"—this was all said directly above the moaning child—"while tha'z bad, for the sick, to talk ad the bedside, and we can't stay with you and not talk, and we can't go in that front yard; that gate is let open so the doctor he needn' ring and that way excide the patient; and we can't go in the back garden"—they spread their hands and dropped them; the back garden was hopelessly pre-empted.

They went to a parlor window and sat looking and longing for the front gate to swing. They had posted on it in Corinne's minute writing: "No admittance excep on business. Open on account sickness. S. V. P. Don't wring the belle!!!"

Cupid lay very flat on his back, his face turned to the open window. He had ceased to moan. When Mrs. Chester stole to where, by leaning over, she could see his eyes they were closed. She hoped he slept, but sat down in uncertainty rather than risk waking him. In the moonlit garden Aline and Geoffry paced to and fro. To see them his mother would have to stand and lean over the cot, and

135

neither good mothers nor good nurses do that. She kept her seat, anxiously hoping that the moonlight out there would remain soft enough to veil the worn look which daylight betrayed on her son's face whenever he fell into silence.

The talk of the pair was labored. Once they went clear to the bower and turned, without a word. Then Geoffry said: "I know a story I'd like to tell you, though how it would help us in our project—if we now have a project at all—I don't see."

"'Tis of the vieux carré, that story?"

"It's of the vieux carré of the world's heart."

"I think I know it."

"May I not tell it?"

"Yes, you may tell it—although—yes, tell it."

"Well, there was once a beautiful girl, as beautiful in soul as in countenance, and worshipped by a few excellent friends, few only because of conditions in her life that almost wholly exiled her from society. Even so, she had suitors—good, gallant men; not of wealth, yet with good prospects and with gifts more essential. But other conditions seemed, to her, to forbid marriage."

"Yes," Aline interrupted. "Mr. Chester, have you gone in partnership with Mr. Castanado—'Masques et Costumes'? Or would it not be maybe better honor to me—and yourself—to speak——"

"Straight out? Yes, of course. Aline, I've been racking my brain—I still am—and my heart—to divine what it is that separates us. I had come to believe you loved me. I can't quite stifle the conviction yet. I believe that in refusing me you're consciously refusing that which seems to you yourself a worthy source of supreme happiness if it did not threaten the happiness of others dearer than your own."

"Of my aunts, you think?"

"Yes, your aunts."

"Mr. Chester, even if I had no aunts——"

"Yes, I see. That's my new discovery: you've already had my assurance that I'd study their happiness as I would yours, ours, mine; but you think I could never make your aunts and myself happy in the same atmosphere. You believe in me. You believe I have a future that must carry me—would carry us—into a world your aunts don't know and could never learn."

"'Tis true. And yet even if my aunts——"

"Had no existence—yes, I know. I know what you think would still remain. You can't hint it, for you think I would promptly promise the impossible, as lovers so easily do. Aline, I would not! 'Twouldn't be impossible. It shall not be. My mother is helping to prove that even to you, isn't she—without knowing it? I promise you as if it were in the marriage contract and we were here signing it, that if you will be my wife I never will, and you never shall, let go, or in any way relax, your hold—or mine—on the intimate friendship of the coterie in Royal Street. They are your inheritance from your father and his father, and I love you the more adoringly because you would sooner break your own heart than forfeit that legacy." He took one of her hands. "You are their 'Clock in the Sky'; you're their 'Angel of the Lord.' And so you shall be till death do you part." He took the other hand, held both.

Cupid turned his face from the window and audibly sobbed.

"Oh, child, what is it? Does it pain so?"

He shook his head.

"Doesn't it pain? Is it not pain at all? Why, then, what is it?"

"Joy," he whispered as the doctor came in.

L

The child's hurts were not so grave, after all.

"He may sit up to-morrow," the doctor said. The fractured arm was put into a splint and sling, and a collar-bone had to be wrapped in place; but the absorbent cotton bandaged on his head was only for contusions.

"Corinne!" Mlle. Yvonne gasped, "contusion"! Ah, doctor, I 'ope tha'z something you can't 'ave but once!"

"You can't in fatal cases. Mrs.—eh—those scissors, please? Thank you."

"Well, Aline, praise be to heaven, any'ow his skull, from ear to ear 'tis solid! Ah, I mean, of co'se, roun' the h-outside. Inside 'tis hollow. But outside it has not a crack! eh, doctor?"

"Except the sutures he was born with. Now, my little man——"

"Ah, ah, Corinne! Born with shuture'! and we never suzpeg' that!"

"Ah, but, Yvonne, if he's had those sinz' that long they cann' be so very fatal, no!"

Partly for the little boy's sake three days were let pass before Aline made her announcement. There was but one place for it—the

Castanados' parlor. All the coterie were there—the De l'Isles, even Ovide—butler pro tem.

"You will have refreshments," he said, with happiest equanimity; "I will serve them"; and the whole race problem vanished. Mélanie too was present, with an announcement of her own which won ecstatic kisses, many of them tear-moistened but all of them glad. As for Mme. Alexandre and Beloiseau, they announced nothing, but every one knew, and said so in the smiling fervency of their hand-grasps.

All of which made the evening too hopelessly old-fashioned to be dwelt on, though one point cannot be overlooked. It was the last proclamation of the joyous hour, and was Chester's. He had bought—on wonderfully easy terms—vieux carré terms—the large house and grounds opposite the Chapdelaine cottage, and there the aunts were to dwell with the young pair.

"Permanently?"

"Ah, only whiles we live!"

The coterie adjourned.

Already the sisters had begun to move in. Mrs. Chester helped them "marvellouzly." Also Aline. Also Cupid—that was now his only name. The cat really couldn't; she was too preoccupied. The sisters touched Mrs. Chester's arm and drew a curtain.

"Look! . . . Eight! Ah, thou unfaithful, if we had ever think you are going to so forget yo'seff like that, we woul'n' never name you Marie Madeleine! And still ad the same time you know, Mrs. Chezter, we are sure she's trying to tell us, right now, that this going to be the laz' time!"

"And me," Yvonne added, "I feel sure any'ow that, as the poet say—I'm prittie sure 'tis the poet say that—she's mo' sin' ag-ainz' than sinning."

At length one evening so many relics of the Chapdelaine infancy had been gathered in the new home that the sisters went over there to pass the night, and took puss and her offspring along. But not a wink did either of them sleep the night through, and the first living creature they espied the next morning was Marie Madeleine, with a kitten in her teeth, moving back.

"Aline," they sobbed as soon as they could find her, "we are sorry, sorry, sorry, to make you such unhappinezz like that, and so soon; continue, you and Geoffry, to live in that new 'ouse; but whiles we live any plaze but heaven we got to live in that home of our infancy."

www.ingramcontent.com/pod-product-compliance
Lightning Source LLC
Chambersburg PA
CBHW011513170626
46810CB00009B/3353